Praise for
The Girl Who Stole an Elephant

Praise for
The Boy Who Met a Whale

Indie Children's Book of the Month, *Financial Times* Best
Children's Books of the Year, BookTrust Great Books Guide

"Another brilliant adventure." – *The Week Junior*

"Danger, bravery, cunning and knife-edge tension compete
in this thriller, enhanced by the rich backdrop of the Indian
Ocean." – *Daily Mail*

"A gripping maritime adventure ... its sunswept sweetness and
tempestuous pace make for a delicious 'book holiday'."
– *Guardian*

"*The Boy Who Met a Whale* has it all: menace, mayhem, majestic
sea creatures and even a melancholic ox whose dreams of
finding adventure are hilariously fulfilled. I absolutely loved
it!" – Hana Tooke, author of *The Unadoptables*

"Edge-of-seat thrills contrast with the beauty and wildlife of
a remote island nation as three youngsters must use their wits
and determination to rescue lost treasure and escape a pair of
murderous criminals." – BookTrust Great Books Guide

"There's fast-paced action, oodles of peril, heartfelt friendship
and a joyful sense of wonder at the natural world." – *Bookseller*

"Another brilliant escapade, jam-packed with peril,
kidnapping, missing treasure and a huge blue whale." –
Scholastic Book of the Month

"A thrilling and fast-paced read which will leave you
breathless." – *Scotsman*

Praise for
The Girl Who Lost a Leopard

Waterstones Best Children's Fiction of the Year, Junior Library
Guild Gold Standard Selection

"Full of peril, heart-stopping adventure & a leopard you'll
fall in love with ... this book is utterly brilliant. With a
conservation theme, it's not only suited to the classroom, it's
perfect for animal & nature lovers." – Hannah Gold, author of
The Last Bear

"A tale for those who crave animal adventures such as those of
Lauren St John and Katherine Rundell ... Outstanding."
– New Statesman

"Edge-of-your-seat excitement." *– Daily Mail*

"A fast-paced roller coaster that will hold readers spellbound."
– Julia Eccleshare

"Nizrana Farook writes quite simply the BEST action-
adventure novels for kids ... I enjoyed every moment of it."
– Stephanie Burgis, author of *The Dragon With a
Chocolate Heart*

"Pacy, gripping writing with extraordinary, atmospheric world-
building ... WOW. And the wonder of it all. A girl who runs
with a leopard! You need this book." – Rashmi Sirdeshpande,
author of *Dadaji's Paintbrush*

"Will leave you hanging at the edge of your seat ... or in this
case off a cliff edge!!" – A.M. Dassu, author of *Boy, Everywhere*

Nizrana writes so exquisitely ... a sheer joy to read!"
– Nicola Penfold, author of *Where the World Turns Wild*

THE BOY WHO SAVED a BEAR

Have you read these other adventures set on the amazing island of Serendib?

THE GIRL WHO STOLE an ELEPHANT

THE BOY WHO MET a WHALE

THE GIRL WHO LOST a LEOPARD

THE BOY WHO SAVED a BEAR

NIZRANA FAROOK

nosy
crow

First published in the UK in 2023 by Nosy Crow Ltd
Wheat Wharf, 27a Shad Thames,
London, SE1 2XZ, UK

Nosy Crow Eireann Ltd
44 Orchard Grove, Kenmare,
Co Kerry, V93 FY22, Ireland

Nosy Crow and associated logos are trademarks and/or registered
trademarks of Nosy Crow Ltd

ISBN: 978 1 83994 392 8

A CIP catalogue record for this book will be available from the
British Library.

Printed and bound in Great Britain by Clays Ltd, Elcograf S.p.A.
Typeset by Tiger Media

Papers used by Nosy Crow are made from wood grown in
sustainable forests.

MIX
Paper from
responsible sources
FSC® C018072

1 3 5 7 9 10 8 6 4 2

www.nosycrow.com

To everyone who has been a part of this journey.

From the trumpeting of a loveable elephant
And the singing of a majestic whale,
To the roar of a noble leopard
And the paw-pad of an enchanting bear.

Thank you for coming along.

MAP of SERENDIB

Great Library of the North

North Road

PORT

KING'S CITY

Royal Complex

Temple

Town and Market

Nirissa

River

Villages

High Road

HANTHANA MOUNTAINS

Turtle Beach

GALLE

Elephant Rock

N

Chapter One

The grandest elephants in the country stood on the lawn of the Great Library of the North.

Nuwan skidded to a halt in the shadows of the palmyra trees, watching the hustle and bustle with excitement. Mahouts fussed over their elephants on the green in front of the triple-domed white brick library building. The elephants were all sizes – mostly huge but some smaller ones too – and there was even one tiny little elephant, standing there swaying softly as musicians tested their instruments. The elephants were dressed in their finest garb, ready for the procession that was to come.

Nuwan looked around him. A crowd had gathered to watch and a thrilling expectation was in the air. Groups of people stood dotted about in the shade of the trees on the edge of the lawn.

"Hey, Nuwan!" said a voice from his left, and he turned to find one of his friends, Sani, standing with her family. She broke away and ran over to him, her two tight plaits jiggling on her shoulders. "Came to see the elephants too?"

"Yes!" he said. "Aren't they marvellous? The big one is the Queen's!"

Sani beamed. "I know! And my father said he's been entrusted to carry the Key of Nissanka. Apparently it's really valuable and all that. Imagine having such a huge job."

"Looks like he's up to all that pressure!" Nuwan grinned as he eyed the massive elephant and his powerful tusks. A mahout threw the animal a plantain, which he caught expertly in his trunk. The embellishments on his regalia winked in the blistering sunlight.

"What's going on?" Another of their friends, Chathura, came up to them under the palmyra trees, munching on something. He had a paper cone of boiled cashew nuts, which he offered to them. "My father dragged me here but I'm not sure what's happening."

Nuwan laughed as he threw a handful of cashews into his mouth. "That's because you're napping most of the time."

Sani giggled and Chathura grinned sheepishly. The crowd pressed forwards and an official waved them back bossily.

"So, Chathura, you know there's this huge old statue in the King's City from the time of King Nissanka?" began Nuwan, but Sani jumped in.

"Legend says that the king didn't trust his successor, so he had the statue built with a cavity where he could hide his treasure and keep it safe for the future," she said. "You can sort of see hinges and a lock apparently, but no one knew if a key to the treasure trove actually existed."

"People have tried to break in over the years," said Nuwan, craning his neck over the elephants to see if there was any activity in the library building. "They never succeeded. But now they've found the key."

Chathura's eyes widened. "And it was *here* all along? Miles away from the King's City?"

Nuwan nodded and took another mouthful of the tender cashews. "One of the junior staff cleaning the archives found the key among a lot of junk. It was checked by experts and it's genuine."

"So what's that got to do with all the elephants?"

"The Queen's going to open the statue! The elephants are carrying the key to her in a procession that'll take five days. They're going to go slowly through towns along the way and rest at night. On Saturday evening there's a ceremony where the key will be handed over to the Queen."

Chathura started fanning himself with the now empty paper cone. The heat was intense and Nuwan welcomed the slight breeze from it.

"I wish I could see it," said Sani wistfully. "The actual key, I mean. Rather than just the box it'll be in, and from this distance too!"

All three of them stared across at the library building, where officials were going in and out as they got ready for the handover.

"That would be so amazing if we could." Chathura turned to Nuwan. "Pity your brother, Krishnan, isn't here. He works at the library, doesn't he?"

"Oh yes!" said Sani. "If only he were here."

"He doesn't *work* at the library," said Nuwan, a

little resentfully. Krish was a sore point with him. His brother was the golden child of the family and sometimes Nuwan wished everybody didn't *need* him quite so much. "He does a monthly delivery of library books to a monk at the King's City. I wouldn't call that working here."

"Still," said Sani. "If he were here he'd go in to see and tell us all about it."

"Well, he's not here," Nuwan said curtly, "even though he was supposed to do a delivery today. He's been ill for the last few days. So he's no good to us."

He paused. An idea glimmered in his mind. This was serendipitous timing. Krish wasn't here so he couldn't do his job. But Nuwan *was* here... He could do Krish's delivery! He would get to see the Key of Nissanka *and* prove to his parents, and everyone else, that he was as capable as his brother.

"You know what," he said to the others, "I think I'm going inside."

Chapter Two

"What?" said Sani to Nuwan. "You can't do that. They'll kick you out."

"No, they won't. I'm going to do Krish's job for him this one time because he's not well."

Chathura frowned. "They're not going to believe that you can do it."

"Why not?" said Nuwan. "It's just a matter of taking a few books to the King's City and giving them to the monk at a temple. My brother does it every month."

"It's a two-day journey to the King's City!" Sani sighed. "Krishnan is sixteen.

You're twelve. Your parents won't let you go."

"My brother's been doing it since he was my age. I don't see why I can't." Nuwan bristled inside at his friends' lack of confidence in him. They were just like his parents!

"Nuwan, wait!" Sani called after him as he made his way through the crowd towards the library. More people had gathered now. He ducked behind a man carrying a child on his shoulders so she could see better and went towards the sweeping drive.

"What are you doing?" An icy voice behind him made Nuwan jump out of his skin. He whipped round and found Mrs Weerasinghe, the head librarian, staring at him.

"I'm here to pick up some books that have been reserved for delivery to the King's City," he said, making his voice sound mature and responsible.

"Today's not the day for that sort of thing. Who are you?" she said again, in a tone somewhere between surprised and annoyed. Her grey-streaked hair was tied up in a tight bun and she wore a stiffly draped sari pinned down severely. "And why do you look like Krishnan, the usual delivery boy?" She looked him up and down unfavourably. "Except smaller and messier."

"Krish is my brother," said Nuwan, ignoring the sting. Krish had talked about Mrs Weerasinghe, and not in a complimentary way. She was new and secretly disliked by other library staff. "He's sick, so I'm delivering the books for him."

"This is highly irregular." She muttered something under her breath. "Not to mention bad timing. Come back tomorrow."

"B-but," stammered Nuwan. "My brother said it was really important. The monk, Mahanama, will be waiting for his book delivery. My brother always takes a new batch on the first of every month." The first part wasn't strictly true, but at least the second was.

Mrs Weerasinghe scowled at him. "How old are you?"

"Twelve. Apart from that, me and Krish are basically the same person. Although I *am* better looking."

She stared at him and he debated whether to let her know that he was joking. "Oh, all right then. But hurry up. Take it and go! As if I don't have enough things to worry about today."

Nuwan smiled in relief as she stalked away. This was going to be easier than he'd thought. He kept well behind her erect figure as she disappeared into the whitewashed building. Now, if anyone asked, he could tell people he had Mrs Weerasinghe's permission!

He left behind the hustle and bustle of the lawn and stepped into the library. It was quiet and dark after the brightness of outside. Nuwan made sure to wipe his feet hard on the coir rug and went in. Some library staff hurried about, ignoring him. There was a large, U-shaped counter and beyond he could see shelves of books. Some of them looked old and leather-bound, while some were shelved horizontally with long, narrow palm-leaf pages. The building was old and cavernous and had a faint whiff of dust that made his nose tickle.

Where was the Key of Nissanka?

Someone jostled against him. "Out of the way!" said a man, hurrying past.

"Excuse *me!*" said Nuwan, stepping back behind the library counter. Mrs Weerasinghe was nowhere to be seen, thankfully. A man and a woman stood at the front of the counter, in a hushed discussion with someone official on the other side.

Nuwan's eyes fell to a small stack of books behind the counter. He tried to read the titles from where he was standing. A couple of the volumes were in another language but he noticed a science book among them. He remembered Krish mentioning that the monk he delivered books to read works of science mostly. Maybe these were his?

"Hello?" said Nuwan. But either the adults didn't hear him or they were ignoring him. Nuwan looked around but everybody seemed incredibly busy and important. Was he supposed to just take the books and leave? Should he ask someone first? He went and picked up the books, and the three adults still didn't seem to notice him. He stood there for a moment, books in hand, hoping that someone would speak to him. But nobody did so he went round the counter, seeing if he could spot any sign of the key.

"Right, is everything ready then?" Mrs Weerasinghe suddenly strode up to the counter, arms swinging by her sides. Instinctively, Nuwan stepped back into the shadows. Mrs Weerasinghe's face was hard and angry, with deep lines all down it.

A few officials gathered around and one brought out a silver box. She opened the lid while Mrs Weerasinghe laid a thick pouch on the counter. Reaching inside, she carefully took out an old metal key. It was large and dark with age, with three decorative loops spiralling round the top. Everyone leaned in closer and seemed to hold their breath as Mrs Weerasinghe gently laid the key into the velvet-lined interior of the box.

Luckily for Nuwan, everyone's eyes were on the key so he could creep forward unnoticed and have a good look. The woman with the silver box then handed it to a man standing behind her. Nuwan recognised him as the chief of their town.

The people in front of Nuwan began to disperse so he stepped back into the shadows again quickly. There was a little alcove, barely big enough for a person, into which he pressed himself. The alcove smelled of nelli and sandalwood. Nuwan rearranged the stack of books more securely in his arms and peeped out. All the staff had moved to the entrance of the building. It must be time for the parade to leave.

Well, that was something! He couldn't wait to go and tell Sani and Chathura.

As Nuwan was about to leave the alcove, something caught his eye. It was a book wedged tightly in a space between wooden panels. Nuwan balanced his books on one arm and pulled it out carefully.

It was a volume of poetry. There was a sketch of flowers dropping down from a branch and a title in looping lettering. He didn't understand why it had been put there – maybe someone had forgotten it. He headed towards the counter and was about to leave it when he changed his mind.

The monk probably liked poetry too. And it would be something for Nuwan to read on the long journey to the King's City. He added the book to his stack and turned to leave.

"Who are you?" A woman was staring at him with concern in her eyes. She was still behind the counter even though everyone else had gone outside. "What were you doing over there?"

"Oh … just, um." Nuwan tried to think of something but his mind went blank. Eventually he stammered, "I-I was j-just collecting some books for a delivery." Then he hurried off before she could say anything else.

A great burst of music reached him when he got to the steps. The elephants were in a line now, smallest at the front and biggest at the back. The Queen's elephant had a silver cage-like object on his back. Music from the hewisi band floated around, giving the whole place a carnival atmosphere as drummers strutted and beat in time. The drumbeat grew faster and louder and Nuwan hurried closer to see what was going on.

The chief held the silver box, with the library staff standing in a line behind him. Nuwan could just about make out the red interior and caught a tiny glimpse of the Key of Nissanka nestled inside. He felt thrilled that he'd seen it close up. The chief handed the box over to an official of the Queen. The official looked at it and nodded, before closing the box. As the music swelled, the Queen's elephant knelt down and the official placed the box in the cage on its back and locked it.

The crowd cheered. The key had been handed over and was on its way to the palace. The crowd of onlookers followed in delight as the elephants started walking away.

Nuwan stood on the lawn and watched as the crowd disappeared into the distance, following the procession, and the music faded away.

Sani or Chathura weren't anywhere in sight, but he didn't mind. He'd go and see them later and tell them all about what had happened!

Nuwan smiled in anticipation. Now he had a delivery to make. And finally he would get to prove himself. But as he made his way home, the strangest feeling came over him. The books in his arms felt heavier and heavier, as if he was carrying something terrible away with him.

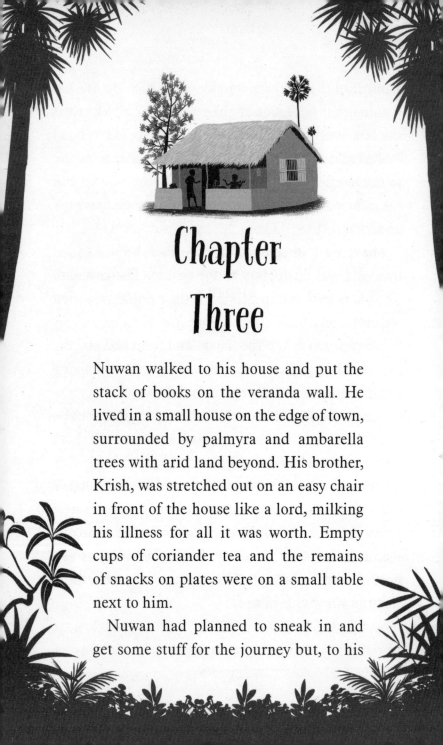

Chapter Three

Nuwan walked to his house and put the stack of books on the veranda wall. He lived in a small house on the edge of town, surrounded by palmyra and ambarella trees with arid land beyond. His brother, Krish, was stretched out on an easy chair in front of the house like a lord, milking his illness for all it was worth. Empty cups of coriander tea and the remains of snacks on plates were on a small table next to him.

Nuwan had planned to sneak in and get some stuff for the journey but, to his annoyance, Krish spotted him.

"Are those *library books*?" he said, sitting up when he saw Nuwan. "What are you doing with them?"

Nuwan braced himself. "I'm doing you a favour and delivering them this month."

Krish stared at him in amazement, his mouth frozen in shock. Then he screamed, "MOTHER! Come here!"

"Don't call her! There's no need for the drama!" Nuwan rolled his eyes.

But Mother came running at once, almost falling in her haste to get to Krish. "What is it, son? Are you all right?"

"Of course he's all right!" said Nuwan angrily, gesturing at the empty plates by his brother. "How else would he stuff all that food into himself?"

But Mother shushed him and looked at Krish in concern. He gave her a brave smile, as if he'd endured so much but was struggling through.

"As Krish is so sick," said Nuwan, trying not to sound sarcastic, "I'm going to deliver the books from the library to the King's City." He thought it was best to get in before Krish did.

"You!" Mother put down Nuwan's sister, Priya, who was hanging from her hip. She went scampering away after the cat, her dress flying out behind her. "Don't be silly, Nuwan. Krishnan will take care of it when he's better."

"No! *I'll* take care of it now." Nuwan was determined to do this.

"You won't." Mother was growing impatient. "This is no job for you. I thought you went to the library to see the elephants?"

"I did. But then I thought I'd do Krish this favour too."

Krish spluttered in indignation. "I don't need any favours."

"Stop bickering, the pair of you," said Mother. "Go and get some water from the well, Nuwan."

"Why can't I do this?" wailed Nuwan. "You and Father never give me a chance!"

Mother looked startled. "Now that's just not true. You're not ready for it, that's all."

"Krish started this job when he was my age! I'll only be gone for four days. Two days there and two back."

Father came out, drying his hands on a cloth. "What's all the commotion?"

"It's Nuwan," said Krish, from his lordly position on the easy chair. "He thinks he should be allowed to go to the King's City by himself."

Father frowned. "Certainly not. You'd have to walk along lonely roads, sometimes through forests, for hours on end. There's a drought on and many of the wild animals will have come out of the forests in search of water. It's simply too dangerous."

"But—"

"No buts," said Mother firmly. "You know what we think. This conversation is over. Now, I have to go make that ponyfish soup for Krish. The poor dear needs to build up his strength."

From the easy chair, Krish smiled smugly at Nuwan. "Thank you, Mother," he said, his voice weak and shaky.

Nuwan clenched his fist. He had a good mind to throw the ponyfish soup on his brother's head.

Father went back in the house and Mother retreated to her soup making. As soon as they'd gone, Krish stretched and laughed. "It's the right decision. We all know you can't do something like this. You'd mess up. You always do."

Nuwan stamped into the house. *None* of his family *ever* believed in him. Well, he was more determined than ever.

He was going on this journey.

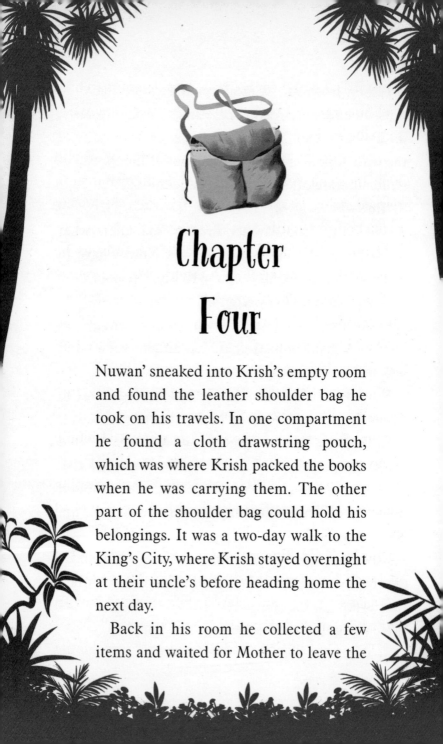

Chapter Four

Nuwan' sneaked into Krish's empty room and found the leather shoulder bag he took on his travels. In one compartment he found a cloth drawstring pouch, which was where Krish packed the books when he was carrying them. The other part of the shoulder bag could hold his belongings. It was a two-day walk to the King's City, where Krish stayed overnight at their uncle's before heading home the next day.

Back in his room he collected a few items and waited for Mother to leave the kitchen. He could hear her pottering about for a while, then she went out with a cup of the blasted ponyfish soup for Krish.

Nuwan slipped into the kitchen and looked around him. In a pan near the hearth he found a bunch of roasted palmyra sprouts and a few slabs of honey-soaked peanut brittle.

"Hmm." He chewed his nail thoughtfully as he looked around the kitchen at the fire-blackened clay pots and coconut-shell spoons. Would these snacks be enough? What did Krish take?

Didn't matter, he'd have to improvise and find things to eat along the way.

Nuwan put the bag back in his room, then sauntered casually on to the verandah.

"I'm going to Sani's house," he announced loudly to no one in particular.

"Don't shout," said Krish annoyingly, now sipping the soup with a pained look on his face. "My head can't take all the noise."

"Be back for dinner, Nuwan," said Mother. "I'm making your favourite brinjal and drumstick curry."

"That's not *my* favourite!" said Nuwan incredulously. "It's Krish's!"

"Oh." She busied herself suddenly, collecting

empty plates. "Tomorrow I'll do … er, yours." She disappeared back into the house.

Nuwan groaned under his breath. He stalked off to his room and collected the packed bag. He waited till Mother had gone to Krish and crept out through the kitchen door. Slinging the bag over his shoulder he set off on his journey, his family's faithless words ringing in his ears as he went.

He hadn't got very far when he realised he'd like someone along on the journey. It would be nice to have some company. And he hadn't even told Sani and Chathura about the key!

But who? Chathura was probably napping so he'd go and ask Sani. She was brave and fun and would be more than ready for the challenge.

That was settled then. He was making good decisions already! Nuwan felt a burst of pride as he made his way to Sani's.

Chapter
Five

Nuwan walked down the path with a spring in his step, his bag of books thudding against his side. The sun was high in the sky, making him perspire slightly, but nothing could dampen his spirits.

He'd done it! He was on his big journey at last. He was going to prove to his family that he was capable of anything.

On the way he passed a sapodilla tree, its branches laden with fruit. He put the bag down and climbed the tree, picking as many fruit as he could. He deliberately chose some that were slightly raw so that they'd ripen over the course of the journey and last longer. He put them in his bag and carried on walking.

At Sani's house, her mother was sitting outside on a bench, feeding rice to a toddler. "Hello, Nuwan," she said, then shouted into the house, "Sani! Nuwan's here."

He smiled at her but she was already distracted. "Come on, now," she said to Sani's little brother, coaxing food into the baby's mouth. "Eat it, or you know who will be here. *KARADI!*" She said the last word ominously, opening her eyes wide while the child squealed and ate a mouthful of rice.

Nuwan caught her eye and smiled. That old story! Everyone talked about Karadi, a ferocious wild bear who lived in the forest close by. She'd lashed out at travellers and left them with deep gashes, and, it was rumoured, even worse. Nuwan's cousin said that he knew someone who suffered with daily nightmares after an encounter with her.

Nuwan made a mental note to keep to the road. Karadi didn't sound very pleasant! But no doubt she was just a story cooked up by parents to make their children behave. Karadi was supposed to have a splash of white on her left paw that marked her out from all the other sloth bears in the forest. Well, that and the fact that she was a killer bear. He shrugged to himself. He'd keep to the road and it would all be fine. He wasn't about to let a made-up bear stop him.

Sani met him in the yard outside. "What happened?" she asked. "Did you go inside the library? We couldn't find you and then we had to leave."

"I did go inside!" answered Nuwan, triumphantly. "I saw the Key being put in its box and handed over to the Queen's official and everything. I was *right there* when it was happening."

Sani squealed, but then her eyes fell on his bag and her smile vanished. "Wait, wait! You're actually going to the King's City?"

"Of course," he said. Why did nobody have any faith in him?

Sani shook her head and her two plaits swung from side to side as her face scrunched up. "All by yourself?"

"All by myself." He looked over Sani's shoulder furtively but her mum was telling more fearsome Karadi stories while her little brother was hanging on every word. "And you, if you want to come."

Sani stared at him for a moment. "Let me get this straight. You're going on a four-day journey to the King's City and you want me to come with you?"

"Yes! It'll be an adventure. I thought you'd want to."

"It's too dangerous. I'm surprised your parents let you."

"Well…"

"Oh, *come on.*" Sani looked at him with great disappointment.

Nuwan was crushed. He felt like she'd put a dampener on his trip before he'd even started. "Fine! Don't come. Your loss."

"Nuwan!" called out Sani as he turned and walked away.

But he ignored her and walked on, not breaking stride as he left. He waved at her over his shoulder, leaving Sani's mother and brother to their bear stories and Sani standing there helplessly.

She went to follow him for a moment but stopped. "Be careful!" she called out. "Keep to the road, take breaks in the shade, space out your food and water."

Nuwan grinned to himself. "OK, Grandma," he shouted over his shoulder. He could never stay mad with Sani for long. "See you when I'm back."

There. Everything was set. Nuwan's journey had begun.

Chapter Six

Nuwan wiped his brow as he went. His shirt had already started to stick to his back. He had plenty of water in his bottle but he had to be careful with it as he might not find more easily. Here and there the red soil of the parched earth was cracked into segments like a tray of kiribath. Palmyra trees swished over him and shed wispy needles to the ground.

At midday he stopped and rested under an ironwood tree, grateful for the shade. He smiled. He'd made good progress. Sani not coming was a temporary setback, but it was fine.

He pulled out his lunch of palmyra sprouts from the top of his bag. He wished he had a proper meal for the first day at least, like Mother made for Krish.

He leaned back against the tree and crunched a bite of the hard sprout.

He watched a squirrel bob about the sun-dappled ground and he threw it a piece. The squirrel snatched it and ran up the nearest tree.

Something rustled behind Nuwan. He stiffened, shifted, and looked behind him.

There was nothing there.

"Er, hello?" he said.

Everything was still except for the crack-crack of thorny branches shaking in the breeze.

Maybe it was a small animal passing by, he thought.

"It's nothing!" he told himself. To take his mind off things he pulled out some of the books from the bag. The science book had some interesting diagrams. He flicked through the pages while he munched on the stick of palmyra sprout.

Then he picked up the book of poetry and to his surprise it fell open at a well-worn page.

Nuwan stared at the page in horror. A square had been cut out in the middle, forming a cavity through half of the book.

But that wasn't what had horrified him. He clapped his hand over his mouth. Inside the cut-out space was a small object, cleverly hidden away from sight.

It was a key.

But not just any key. It was the Key of Nissanka that was supposed to be in the procession of elephants on the way to the Queen at that very moment.

Chapter Seven

Nuwan threw the book away from him as if it were something dangerous. He put his head in his hands. Then, groaning, he staggered to his feet. How on earth did any of this make sense?

The key lay on the red soil where it had fallen. Nuwan looked around him. A gust of wind whistled through the trees, dropping leaves on the ground and rustling the pages of the open book.

Nuwan groaned again and rubbed his eyes. What had happened? For some inexplicable reason, he had the most important key in the kingdom in his possession. The key that was meant for the Queen. It was all a terrible mistake.

He picked up the key and wiped the sand off with his shirt. It was heavier than it looked. He placed it back inside the book cavity and frowned.

This was no mistake. The key had been deliberately hidden. And so had the book, tucked, as it had been, into the little alcove. Someone had wanted to smuggle the key away without anyone knowing.

"But I saw the key being handed over!" said Nuwan aloud. The squirrel from earlier came back and looked at him hopefully. He threw it another piece of palmyra sprout.

The feel of the key in his hand chilled him to the bone. If the Key of Nissanka had been put in the silver box and given to the chief right in front of his eyes, what was *this* key, hidden so carefully in the poetry book in the alcove?

The keys were identical as far as he could tell. Which meant one of them was a fake. And it didn't take much for Nuwan to figure out that the real Key of Nissanka had to be the one in his palm right now.

He shivered and felt sick.

There was a sound from the road and Nuwan

quickly stuffed the books back into his bag, looking around worriedly. If someone were to come and find him right now, they'd think that *he* was the thief.

He crept up to the road and watched from behind a tree. He sighed with relief when he realised that it was just a carriage passing through, its wheels trundling along the narrow track.

What should he do now?

"Right," Nuwan said to himself, collecting up his discarded lunch from the ground. He wrapped up the remaining palmyra sprouts in a piece of paper. "I'll just have to take the key back to the library. That's the answer." He was still terrified about handling an object of such importance, but all he had to do was take it back safely. Easy.

Nuwan gathered up all his things and turned back towards town. As he approached the road, he saw an ox cart coming at speed towards him. He stepped back quickly before he got run over. Whoever it was inside was in a mighty hurry.

The cart passed him, stopped, and two people jumped out. A man came racing towards him, followed by a prim woman in a sari. She walked slowly but purposefully, a stern look on her face.

It was Mrs Weerasinghe.

"Hand it over," said the man, nodding towards Nuwan's bag.

"Hand what over?" he said. How could they know he had the key?

The man rolled his eyes and gestured impatiently. "Come on."

Nuwan looked from him to Mrs Weerasinghe. She stared at him with an inscrutable expression. "You have one last chance," she said, "to hand it over to Mr Weerasinghe."

Nuwan took the bag off his shoulder and began to open it, stalling for time. Something nagged at him. How were the pair of them involved in this? *What was going on?*

He paused in the act of taking out the book and looked up. Could he trust them?

Mr Weerasinghe sighed impatiently.

"Take it from him," said Mrs Weerasinghe.

Mr Weerasinghe lunged at Nuwan, trying to grab the bag.

Nuwan reacted instinctively. He slipped out of the man's reach, shouldered the bag, and ran away as fast as he could.

Chapter Eight

Nuwan thundered through the wilderness, brushing past prickly bushes that pulled at his clothes. Mr Weerasinghe was hot on his heels, thumping along with surprising speed. Nuwan couldn't see where Mrs Weerasinghe was, he was so intent on running away. Where and why, he just wasn't sure. All he knew was that something was terribly wrong and he had to get away from the couple. And keep the key safe from them.

There was a crashing sound behind him as Mr Weerasinghe tripped and landed unceremoniously on his face. Nuwan stopped to see him picking himself up, his hands scratched and bleeding.

While the man was distracted, Nuwan sprinted away and jumped over a fallen tree stump. He needed somewhere to hide so that he could get the man off his back.

Something dark loomed up in front of him. A cave!

Nuwan ran over to its craggy mouth. He had to bend slightly to scramble inside. It was pitch dark in there. He leaned against the wall, trying to silence his panting. After the bright sunshine outside he could see nothing. He took his bag off his shoulder and dropped it at his feet.

"Phew," he said to himself. His heartbeat felt like it was echoing noisily through the forest.

He pressed himself to the cool, hard rock as the sound of Mr Weerasinghe's footsteps came from outside. The footsteps paused, receded, then came back again. Mr Weerasinghe must be circling the area, wondering where Nuwan had gone.

Suddenly Nuwan became aware of how close Mr Weerasinghe must be. He could hear the man breathing – very loud and laboured, hoarse even. What on earth was he doing? Then came something like a grunt, followed by more hard breathing.

The hair on the back of Nuwan's neck stood up as a terrifying thought occurred to him. His own breathing became shallow and he tried to make himself as invisible as possible.

That didn't sound like Mr Weerasinghe's breathing at all. In fact, it didn't sound like the breathing of any human. Nuwan turned his head slowly towards the inside of the cave. His eyes had adjusted to the light by now and he could see quite clearly. Standing on its hind legs just a few feet away was a bear.

Chapter Nine

Nuwan froze in fear. The bear stood there, dark and threatening, its outline picked out in the daylight seeping into the cave. Its breath rattled in its throat.

Nuwan's legs wouldn't move. Every hair on his body stood up and his brain urged him to run, but he was rooted to the spot. A bear! An actual live bear, standing in front of him.

Even if he'd wanted to scream, his throat had closed up with fear. He stared in frozen horror at the spectacle of the shaggy, fearsome animal, and then his eyes fell to the patch of brilliant white on its left leg.

It was Karadi.

"I saw the boy come this way," said a man's voice outside the cave, jolting Nuwan out of his shock.

"He's bound to be close, then!" replied Mrs Weerasinghe's voice.

Nuwan's brain froze again, not able to work out how to deal with the twin threats of his human enemies and that of a great big bear.

Karadi snuffled and took a step towards him. She smelled pungent and sweaty. Her fur was jet black and shaggy around her head, and her nose was long and pointed. Nuwan was overcome with terror now – he couldn't think, he couldn't breathe, he felt faint with fright as he flattened himself against the cave wall and willed it to open up behind him. All he could focus on was the fat, pointed nose and fierce bear face under the bushy round ears. Even against his will, his eyes travelled to her claws. His heart clenched at the sight of them, five on each paw, long and curling downwards towards the ground.

"Don't!" came Mrs Weerasinghe's voice, sharply. She sounded right outside now. There was a shuffling at the mouth of the cave. Mr Weerasinghe must have been trying to enter because his wife said, "That's a bear cave! Look at the prints. He wouldn't be stupid enough to go in there. Let's get out of here."

Karadi turned her head towards the entrance to the cave. The couple's footsteps pattered away very fast as they moved on, searching for Nuwan.

As it turned out, Nuwan *was* stupid enough to go into a bear cave.

Karadi turned back towards the boy, making him whimper and moan under his breath. *Please spare me*, he thought, though he didn't dare speak the words out loud. Karadi tilted her head slightly and came a bit closer, as if wondering what to do with him. Her small, beady eyes were jewel-bright, and her expression looked both human and primitive at the same time.

This was it. She was going to rip him apart. Not only had he messed up a simple mission but he was also going to get himself killed. And bring shame on his family when the Weerasinghes told everyone he was a thief who'd tried to steal the Key of Nissanka.

Without any warning, Karadi suddenly dropped on to all fours. She turned away from Nuwan and sloped out of the cave as casual as you please. Nuwan watched her leave, his heart hammering painfully in his chest. She slipped easily through the cave entrance. He could see her legs through the low opening as she gambolled outside and then disappeared from sight.

Nuwan crawled forwards on hands and knees, peering out of the cave. He saw a black shape walking away into the distance. He scuttled hurriedly out of the cave, hardly noticing as he scratched his knees and palms on the hard ground. And then he turned and ran and ran and ran. After a few minutes, he stopped and fell to the ground. He was trembling all over and sobbing quietly.

He'd made it. He'd been inside a cave with a bear and lived to tell the tale. But he didn't feel like a hero. All he wanted was a hug from his mother and to get away from this place and Karadi as fast as he could.

He collected his wits and wiped away his tears. He was all right. He hadn't messed up. He could still finish his journey and earn not only the approval and trust of his family but, by delivering the Key of Nissanka, he could show them that he could be a hero as well.

It was then that he realised the most dreadful thing. His bag wasn't with him. He'd left it back at the bear cave. And in it was the Key of Nissanka.

Chapter
Ten

Nuwan groaned and clapped his hands over his mouth. He couldn't believe it. What had he *done*!

"The key!" he wailed. He couldn't lose that. That would be the worst disaster ever. All he'd wanted to do was one thing well, not ruin everything for ever.

Calm down, calm down, he thought. He took some shallow breaths and closed his eyes to relax his racing heart.

He realised, with a thrill of horror, what he had to do.

He had to go back.

Back to the bear cave. He had no choice. The only way to prove he wasn't a thief was to get that key safely to the Queen in time for the ceremony. And there was no way he was going to fail!

He headed back towards the cave, every step heavy with terror. The sun beat down as he made his way under the rustling trees. He couldn't believe his bad luck. He'd been so happy to escape from the bear with his life and yet here he was, walking straight back again. He just had to hope his luck would hold out for a second time.

He kept a watch for the Weerasinghes as he went. They were never going to let him get away with the key, especially now he knew they were involved in its theft. He was sure of it. Why else was the key hidden so craftily in the book, and why did they come after him instead of go to the authorities?

He stopped when he came in sight of the cave, stepping behind a silvery tree trunk pockmarked with ants' nests. He could hear Karadi rustling about inside. He'd wait here till she came out. She was bound to go and look for food at some point.

As it happened, he didn't have to wait long. A snuffling, grunting sound came from the cave and Karadi squeezed through the gap. Even though he had been expecting it, Nuwan had to actively stop himself screaming and running away. He hid behind the tree as Karadi snuffled the ground outside the cave, grunting and nosing at something. Nuwan was transfixed by the length of her claws.

What was he doing! Just as he was readying himself to run before she saw him and tore him to shreds, she lolloped away. Karadi disappeared into the trees, a blob of black bouncing up and down among the dry, crackling foliage.

Nuwan darted out from behind the tree and ducked inside the cave. It was damp and smelled of rotting fruit. Eurgh. He wrinkled his nose as he straightened up and went to where he'd left the bookbag.

It was there! Exactly where he'd left it. A small sapodilla fruit had fallen out but the bag was intact otherwise. He grabbed it by the strap and turned to go.

Chapter Eleven

He peered out cautiously before stepping through the gap. Karadi was nowhere in sight. For a moment he thought he heard a shuffle and stiffened.

But there was silence after that so he hurried away, wanting to put as much distance as possible between himself and Karadi's lair.

He couldn't believe it! *He*, Nuwan, who people thought messed up everything, had just managed to retrieve something important from the cave of a bear! He felt about a foot taller just thinking about it.

Where was Krish to see *this* then!

He peeked into the bag to check that the books and the key were inside, and patted it gratefully. All was well. He had the books. He had the key. Now he had to deliver it personally into the right hands and thwart the devious plans of the Weerasinghes.

But first, he needed to take some precautions. The key was important. Super important. He couldn't risk losing the bag again, or leaving it somewhere. He sat down and slid the books out of the cloth bag they were in. They fell out and thumped on to the hard, dry earth.

Nuwan pulled out the drawstring from the cloth bag and threaded it through the loop at the end of the Key of Nissanka.

He held it up, the key dangling in the middle of the string, then tied the ends into a secure knot. He pulled it over his head and felt the key resting safely on his chest, under his shirt and close to his heart. Now Nuwan was never going to accidentally leave the key anywhere. It was going wherever he went.

Nuwan looked up. It was evening and the day was finally getting cooler. The forest was ablaze with the light of the setting sun. Leaves crackled as he walked on with his bag, the key sitting comfortably under his shirt. He would join the North Road and get back on track to the King's City.

A twig crunched behind him. Nuwan stopped. The hairs on his arms stood up.

There was nothing behind him, only the darkening forest. He bent down slightly and peered through the trees, trying to spot what could have made the noise. Maybe he'd imagined it? He shook his head and turned to go.

Nuwan jumped out of his skin.

Standing in front of him were Mr and Mrs Weerasinghe.

"Well, Nuwan," said the librarian. "Nice to see you again."

"Sorry I can't say the same," he mumbled.

Mrs Weerasinghe laughed. "Getting mouthy, are we?"

Nuwan stared back at her mutinously. Mr Weerasinghe said nothing but approached Nuwan with purpose.

Nuwan took out the bag of books and held it out to Mr Weerasinghe wordlessly. He didn't want to lose it, but if it'd get the couple off his back for a minute maybe he could run away before they realised he still had the key.

Mr Weerasinghe looked delighted, as if he couldn't believe his luck, and greedily reached for the bag. But Mrs Weerasinghe held up a hand.

"We won't be needing those," she said, making Nuwan's heart sink. Mr Weerasinghe's face contorted in confusion.

Nuwan stuffed the books back into the bag on his shoulder. He felt the coldness of the key against his chest. *Please no*, he thought. *She couldn't know, could she?*

"That was a really good place to put it by the way," she said nonchalantly to Nuwan, as if discussing something quite mundane. "You probably thought it'd be quite safe if you wore it like that. But you were wrong and we'd like it back now."

Nuwan stood stock-still. He couldn't give it to them. Not after all this. Not the key.

Without a moment's hesitation, he turned to scarper. Mr Weerasinghe bellowed with rage and pounced, dragging him back by his shirt. Nuwan struggled, trying to slip out of his grasp but the man's grip was too tight.

"That wasn't very wise." Mrs Weerasinghe sighed. Even though they were in the middle of the forest, dressed in a prim little sari, she didn't have a hair out of place. She looked at Mr Weerasinghe. "Come on! Take it off him."

"NO!" said Nuwan, resisting hard, but it was no use. Mr Weerasinghe pulled the fabric chain off Nuwan's head, the key coming with it. He laughed with joy at getting it in his hands, then quickly passed it to Mrs Weerasinghe.

"I'm going to go tell!" said Nuwan furiously, as he struggled to get out of Mr Weerasinghe's grip. "Everyone will know that you have the key and you mean to open the statue yourself and steal everything."

"Oh, I don't think so." Mrs Weerasinghe had the key in the palm of her hand as she gazed at with pride. "You're not going anywhere."

She looked up to enjoy Nuwan's reaction to her threat before her face changed in horror and she staggered backwards, dropping the key in fright. Something was running towards her at it with great speed, teeth bared and grunting fiercely.

Karadi!

Mrs Weerasinghe turned and ran, then her husband let go of Nuwan and took off after her.

Quick as a flash Nuwan picked up the key but Karadi was after him now. He felt her shaggy body graze his back before he screamed and started to run.

His feet slapped on the dry, hard ground and he ran through the trees, hotly pursued by the vicious bear.

He felt her grunts and the power of her paws thudding on the ground as he ran. She was at his back, racing swiftly with him. He screamed, but even that sound sank deep into his throat as he used all his energy for running away as fast as he could. Away from the bounding ball of fur and claws snapping at his legs.

Nuwan felt a tug at his bag and found Karadi's jaws clamped around it. He screamed as the bag swung wildly and some food fell out.

He carried on running between trees and shrubs, his legs pumping on stone and earth and grass, never stopping until at some point he was aware that Karadi was no longer chasing him. She'd turned her attention to something on the ground, so Nuwan ran and ran, getting far away before he stopped.

Exhausted, he fell to the ground at the base of a palmyra tree, collapsing in a heap of hysterical crying. His body shivered violently and he thought he might be sick. He had never been so frightened in his life. He'd thought he was finished back there.

Nuwan realised there was a string hanging from his fist and unclenched his hand. He had been gripping the key so tightly that it had pressed an angry red mark into his skin.

"What was I *thinking?*" he wailed, tears falling on to the key. His body was racked in sobs again. Krish was right. He couldn't do anything.

Nuwan sniffed and wiped his eyes. Some of the sapodilla he was carrying in the shoulder bag had fallen out. He stood up and adjusted the bag over his shoulder, still holding on to the key. All wasn't lost. He could still save things and prove himself to his family.

But—

"Hello again, Nuwan."

Nuwan's head shot up to see Mrs Weerasinghe walking towards him through the forest. Her husband was just behind her, looking beaten-down and nervous, his eyes darting from side to side as he walked. Clearly Nuwan wasn't the only one that Karadi had terrified.

"You didn't think we would just forget about it, did you?" said Mrs Weerasinghe, gesturing to the key in Nuwan's damp hand. "And leave you to take it away? We worked hard for that."

"LEAVE ME ALONE!" Nuwan screamed out before he could stop himself. All of a sudden he wasn't angry or scared. He was exhausted. These two were like leeches and he felt he'd never be rid of them. After the shock of the bear attack and the anxiety about getting the key to the King's City safely, he was spent. What would it take to get them away from him?

"There's no need to shout." Mrs Weerasinghe adjusted the fall of her sari, pleating it just right. She looked him straight in the face. "Sorry, boy. Give it up. You're not going to succeed."

You're not going to succeed. Krish had said the same. His parents thought the same. And suddenly, Nuwan saw red.

"I WILL succeed!" he screamed at the pair of them. "I will NEVER let you have the key. *Never!*"

He jumped away and ran between the two of them, his anger making him fast and nimble. Mr Weerasinghe swore and began to follow him as he brushed through thorny shrubs and scratched his legs all over again.

Nuwan knew exactly what to do. The problem was that the Weerasinghes weren't afraid of him. But he knew someone – or something – they were terrified of.

Chapter Twelve

Nuwan sprinted towards the bear cave, the adrenaline carrying him forwards. The Weerasinghes were not far behind. Nuwan felt lightheaded and reckless as he ran. He was going to win no matter what. He was *never* giving up the key until he placed it into the Queen's hand!

When he was in sight of the cave, he saw a furry black shape outside. Karadi turned towards the boy expectantly, as if she'd been waiting for him.

Behind him, Mr Weerasinghe stopped. "What are you doing, you mad boy?" he hissed. Mrs Weerasinghe had halted too. She stared with interest at Nuwan.

"Don't come any closer!" Nuwan whispered back. He turned to check what Karadi was doing.

Karadi shifted, then stood up on her hind legs.

Nuwan swallowed down the scream. Behind him, Mr Weerasinghe stepped back, breathing heavily. Only Mrs Weerasinghe stayed still, though Nuwan could see the alarm in her eyes.

"Go away, then!" Nuwan whispered to the couple. "Stop pestering me, or I'll go closer."

"What are you trying to do?" said Mr Weerasinghe. "Give the key back."

"NO," said Nuwan. "I'm going to expose you for what you are."

"There's no use, boy," said Mrs Weerasinghe, also in a lowered voice. "The game is up. It's you who's been exposed."

Nuwan looked back and scoffed. He wasn't going to fall for such nonsense.

"It's true." Mr Weerasinghe crept a little closer but stopped as soon as Nuwan moved too. "Listen. We've been to see your parents. We've told them that you've made off with something valuable. The next step will be the authorities. And we'll tell them that a young boy who wasn't meant to be at the library came in and made off with the key. You know what the authorities will think? That it was all planned by you and your brother."

Nuwan froze. He stared at the two of them, Karadi forgotten.

"Your family aren't too pleased," said Mrs Weerasinghe casually. "You're going to make them the pariahs of the town."

Even with the heat and dryness of the day, Nuwan began to go cold. All he'd wanted was for his family to be proud of him. But to think that he had made things so much worse for them and now they'd be shamed in front of everyone they knew!

"Give us the key then, boy," said Mr Weerasinghe, edging closer.

Nuwan clutched the key and stared at it. His head was too fuzzy to think. He was in over his head already and everything had changed. Would handing over the key make things better or worse?

"We're wasting time," said Mrs Weerasinghe to her husband, sharply. "Take it and let's get out of here."

Karadi watched the argument with interest from her spot in the distance. She took a step forward.

Nuwan's heart skipped a beat.

Mr Weerasinghe stepped back even further. He glanced back at Mrs Weerasinghe. "I can't."

"Oh very well then," she said impatiently. She walked swiftly forward, giving Mr Weerasinghe a contemptuous look as she passed. She came purposefully towards Nuwan and he realised with a start that she wasn't bluffing.

He made a run for it towards Karadi, going as close as he could until they were staring at each other, eye to eye. He smelled the fruity scent on her. He held his breath and then threw the string with the key dangling from it over her head.

He ran back away from the bear as both Weerasinghes gave shouts of disbelief.

"What have you done, you stupid boy?" cried Mrs Weerasinghe.

Karadi stood there in confusion, standing tall on her back legs. For a moment the string hung lopsidedly on her head, stuck around one ear. Then she shook her head hard and the string slipped neatly around her neck, the key of Nissanka nestling into her furry chest.

With another shake of her head Karadi reared up higher and ROARED, the sound echoing around the trees and striking fear into Nuwan's heart. The

Weerasinghes were already scarpering. Nuwan slung the book bag over his shoulder and ran after them, Karadi thudding on behind.

Chapter
Thirteen

Nuwan felt his lungs would burst as he easily overtook the pair. Karadi seemed to lose interest in the chase and disappeared into the forest. Maybe she couldn't be doing with all the bother.

Nuwan stopped and bent down, panting. He slid to the ground at the foot of a tree and leaned back against its grooved trunk. Opening his bottle, he took a few sips of water, then carefully closed it and put it away. He wasn't even bothered that the Weerasinghes were approaching him. He had nothing to give them now.

"What are you playing at?" said Mrs Weerasinghe, her expression cold and furious.

Nuwan stared at her. She looked as neat as she always did, even after that run through the trees. "I'm sick of you coming after me! You have to go after *her* now, if you dare."

He immediately regretted his words as a cold, calculating look came over the woman's face.

Mr Weerasinghe was staring at his wife curiously. He seemed completely clueless. Nuwan could guess who the brains of the duo was.

"We will," said Mrs Weerasinghe to Nuwan. "Don't you worry about that. Even a ferocious bear isn't going to stand in my way. You'd better pray that we get the key before the duplicate one is discovered."

Nuwan snorted. "Why? What's it to me if you get it?"

"You really didn't think this through, did you?" said Mrs Weerasinghe. "We obviously don't want the attention on *us* if the swap is discovered. I will report you as the thief. In fact, one of the library staff saw you skulking around the shadows and hiding in an alcove when it was closed to the public, so that's quite unfortunate for you."

Mr Weerasinghe chuckled. "Serves you right, boy.

Thought you were being clever, didn't you?"

Nuwan got up slowly from the foot of the tree. He was completely beaten down and flummoxed by what he could do next.

"There's no way that any of us can get that key now," he said.

"Oh, we could," Mrs Weerasinghe laughed. "We have our ways." With a mysterious look at him she began to walk off.

"Stay away from us!" said Mr Weerasinghe, as he followed behind his wife. Nuwan stood there watching them until they were out of sight.

As soon as they were gone he collapsed on the ground, the bag digging painfully into his side. This was it. He had to get that key to the Queen. He couldn't prove that the Weerasinghes were behind everything. Mrs Weerasinghe would be believed, as the respectable librarian, rather than the boy who wasn't meant to be there and who was acting suspiciously on the day of the ceremony. So he had to get the key to the King's City before the swap could be discovered.

It was getting dark and Nuwan was tired. He drank a little more water and lay back against the base of a tree, thinking about his next move. He wasn't really worried about the water situation. If he got back on the road he was sure to find a well for travellers, where hopefully he would be able to refill his bottle. He had bigger things to worry about.

Right at this moment the procession of elephants would be moving through the towns with the Weerasinghes' duplicate key. They were probably getting ready to rest up for the night. It would take five days for them to get to the palace. Which meant Nuwan had four days at most to get the key off Karadi, keep the Weerasinghes at bay, and get to the Queen before the swap was discovered.

He was thinking for a long time as the night darkened around him, the dread lying heavy in his heart. As his eyes closed in sleep he thought fleetingly that bears weren't the only wildlife that could come out at night. But somehow the events of the day overtook him and he fell into a deep sleep.

Chapter
Fourteen

When Nuwan woke up, he stared blearily into the brightening day. A green pigeon cooed continuously over him, its bright hue standing out in the leafless tree.

He rubbed his eyes and got up. He had to figure out what he was going to do quickly; time was ticking by. He hurried to his bag, which he'd discarded on the ground last night, and saw that some animal had been at it. It had been roughly tossed aside and items were spilled out on the ground. The books were safe but there were bits of sapodilla lying nearby, the remnants of someone's supper.

Nuwan scratched his head. It obviously wasn't Mr or Mrs Weerasinghe who had gone through his bag. Unless they were very hungry! He grinned in spite of everything. It had to be an animal. He knelt down and gathered up the books, closing the bag around them securely.

It was when he got up that he noticed the prints.

Bear prints, very close to where he was fast asleep last night. Nuwan rubbed at his eyes in disbelief. This was very strange. Karadi had been here. Right next to him as he slept.

But she'd left him alone.

He massaged his temples as he stood there thinking. She was the most fearsome bear in Serendib – why did she not attack him? Because Nuwan was sleeping perhaps, so she knew he was no threat to her?

But an idea began to form in his mind, making his heart leap with excitement and terror at the same time.

He had to take the key to the King's City if he wanted to fix things for himself and his family. There was no other way. But it was around Karadi's neck. And Nuwan preferred that because it was the safest way of keep it from falling into

Mrs Weerasinghe's grasping hands.

Maybe Karadi wasn't as aggressive as people believed her to be. She'd left him alone last night, hadn't she? Had she eaten the sapodilla?

"What do bears eat anyway?" he said aloud. Things like fruit and termites? Eurgh, termites – hopefully Nuwan would never be mistaken for one. Could Karadi like the taste of sapodilla by any chance?

"Of course!" he thought to himself. Excitement coursed through him. He remembered Karadi chasing after him, grasping at his bag – the bag that contained the sapodilla.

"Oh, Karadi," he said, with a laugh. "I just got it. You weren't attacking me at all. All you wanted was the sapodilla fruit in my bag."

The whole thing seemed so ridiculous that he began to laugh. It was a mixture of amusement and relief, and he bent over and laughed and laughed at finally figuring out Karadi's motives. That first time in the cave Karadi had walked away from Nuwan, perhaps realising he meant her no harm. A sapodilla fruit had fallen from his bag then, too, so maybe that was when she'd got her first taste. And after that, she associated him with delicious food and looked out for him.

The idea in his mind was starting to grow bigger

and bigger. He'd thought of a plan so amazing, so daring, that it would take a special kind of hero to pull it off. No way would Krishnan be up to it!

He held up a sapodilla fruit and smiled. "Oh, Karadi. You've got something I want, and *I've* got something *you* want."

He was completely clear on what he had to do. He was going on a journey to the King's City, accompanied by a wild and ferocious bear.

Chapter Fifteen

Nuwan stopped by a clearing to plan out what he had to do. He *should* have been afraid but he wasn't. He felt completely calm, and even a little bit excited, about the adventure ahead. He was still going to the King's City but he would take Karadi with him, guarding the key all the way. He'd use the sapodilla to entice her.

He picked up a stick and drew his path to the King's City on the ground, scratching out the dry earth.

"I can't go on the North Road now," he said, as he marked out the road and the forest adjoining with little v shapes. "Imagine that, walking down the road with a bear."

He scratched his head as he looked at his rough map.

"This is how Karadi and me should travel," he said. He marked out a route, turning up a thin shaving of earth as he did so. Mrs Weerasinghe would expect him to use the North Road, so he'd have to avoid that and go through the forest to the port instead. Then from there he'd go on to the King's City. But this would mean that instead of two days, it would probably take him about five. And the elephants carrying the fake key would reach the King's City in four. He'd have to go *really* fast!

"Right, first step – find the bear." Nuwan stood up and tried to get his bearings. He knew roughly where Karadi's cave was. He just had to retrace his steps.

He slung his bag over his shoulder and set off, the bag slapping against his side as he moved. The day was still cool at this time of the morning. A lone elephant stood at a drying watering hole, flapping its tail against some insects buzzing on its back.

Nuwan was hoping to come across something to eat before he got to the bear cave. The sapodilla fruit was precious now he was saving it for Karadi. But so was the water, and he needed to find a clean supply for himself soon.

He found some nungu fruit on a tree and grabbed them with glee. The cold fruit sliding down his throat was just the refreshment he needed. He felt as though he'd got his fill of water from it too, as he continued on.

There was Karadi's cave! Nuwan gulped as he approached it slowly.

Where was she?

He didn't want to just run into her. Now that he was here, the fear was creeping up again, like pinpricks of ice through his skin.

He positioned himself behind an unusually leafy bush and peered through the branches, holding the leaves apart with his hands.

All was quiet at the cave. Perhaps she was sleeping. Bears did sleep for most of the day after all. But he had to entice her out of there. He had to get her moving – and fast – so they could reach the Queen before the missing key was discovered.

Nuwan edged up to the cave. His legs had gone weak and he had to will them to move. He stood at the entrance, listening intently. Was that breathing? He crouched even lower, tilting forward slightly and straining to hear.

"WHAAARVE!" came a screech and Nuwan screamed and jerked his head up, hitting it on the cave as he did so. Scrambling backwards, he ran as fast as he could from the cave.

What *was* that noise? That wasn't Karadi!

He stopped and looked around, then groaned when he saw what had made the noise. A grey hornbill was perched on a branch near the cave. It squawked again, the same caw that had made Nuwan jump out of his skin and scared him half to death.

But it looked like Nuwan's screaming and jumping about had disturbed Karadi. A black, furry shape peeked out of the cave before squeezing into the open air. The bear walked languidly and looked around, her eyes coming to rest on Nuwan.

"I can do this," said Nuwan softly. "She's not going to hurt me." Before he tried to befriend the bear, he had to calm himself down. All his instincts were telling him to flee.

Karadi turned around properly to face Nuwan. Sunlight glinted on the key around her neck. He wondered briefly if it bothered her, but she hardly seemed to notice. She came towards him, then stopped.

Nuwan stood his ground.

He could feel a rivulet of sweat trickle down his back but he kept eye contact with the bear.

Her shaggy head tilted a little. He could swear she was thinking.

"Here, Karadi," he said, keeping his voice low so he didn't startle her.

She stood up on her hind legs. A deep-throated grunt came from her.

Nuwan gulped. It was nothing, he told himself. She wasn't that dangerous. She'd been close to him several times but hadn't done anything to him, had she?

He needed to break the barrier between them. Show her he trusted her. "Here, Karadi," he repeated. He clicked his fingers. "Want to come on a journey with me?"

She stared at him with what seemed almost like confusion.

Feeling bolder, Nuwan stepped forward. At which point, Karadi's expression changed. She threw up her head and roared, a sound that thundered through the trees and into Nuwan, making him back away and fall over. She watched him get up and roared again, dropping on to her paws and bounding towards him.

Nuwan turned and fled, his feet pumping in time with his heart as he raced away from Karadi. He sensed her stop almost immediately. It looked like she just wanted him to leave.

Nuwan turned back, looking at her from a distance. Even from here, her expression was one of fury. She roared at him, her head shaking from side to side.

It was a clear message to him. *Get out. And stay out.*

Chapter Sixteen

Nuwan retreated, moving away from Karadi, trying to get well out of her sight. She didn't follow him but watched him warily. Once he was far enough away, he saw her dark shape move back to her cave.

Nuwan carried on, passing his optimistic journey map scratched out on the ground. He sat down by a pile of rocks to think.

Two things came to him. One, he wasn't nearly as afraid of Karadi as he had been. And just then, when she'd turned on him, she didn't seem to *want* to hurt him.

She'd stayed put and warned him off. Two, a barrier of sorts had been broken between them. She'd told him something, and he'd understood.

Obviously the message could have been nicer than, "Stay away, I hate you." But still, it was progress.

"There's something I'm missing," said Nuwan, absently drawing on the ground with his toe. What had made Karadi so mad? For a moment it had looked as though she would come for him. If he was going to befriend her, he had to work out how not to get killed by her as a minimum.

He'd tried to show her that he trusted her. But maybe this wasn't about him. It was about her. Why should *she* trust him? That was what he had to show her first. Precious as it was, was he going to have to give her the sapodilla fruit *without* any expectations?

"I'm going to give you a little time," he said to Karadi, as if she were around and could hear him. "And then try again."

Meanwhile he decided to go to the road and see if he could find a well to refill his bottle. All the rivers had dried up.

When he got to the road, he had to walk down it for about twenty minutes until he found a well. He kept to the trees just in case the Weerasinghes came back.

He paused for a moment as he lifted the handle of the well. Had he put Karadi in danger by making her the guardian of the key now? But the Weerasinghes were certainly too frightened of her to try to mess with her.

He pumped water into the bucket left next to the well, then filled his bottle and wished he had a second one.

He made his way back to where he'd drawn the map on the ground. To his surprise, someone was crouched over it, frowning as if trying hard to make sense of it.

"Sani!" he said.

She whipped round and smiled at him. A fat bag of her own lay on the ground near her.

"Sani!" he said again, coming up. "Wh-what are you doing here?"

"Nuwan!" She jumped up and ran towards him. "You're OK! I've been so worried about you – this woman came to see your parents. She said terrible things about you that can't be true."

"Mrs Weerasinghe," Nuwan said gloomily, tightening the lid on his bottle.

"She said that you'd stolen something really valuable from the library, and if they don't find you and get it back, they're going to the authorities. Your parents are so upset."

He closed his eyes in despair. How could things have gone so wrong?

"Is it true?" she said. "Did you steal something?"

"Of course not! *They* stole something, but I found it and accidentally took it away with me. So now they're after me."

"And there's more," said Sani. "Late last night there was a commotion in the village. Mr Weerasinghe turned up claiming a wild bear had attacked him. Mrs Weerasinghe was furious and reported it to the wildlife authorities and they're going to hunt for it so they can put it down. She said it was out of control and that it should be stopped before it kills someone."

"Oh no!" said Nuwan, his blood running cold. "They can't do that! Karadi hasn't done anything wrong!"

"What?" Sani looked totally confused. "How do you know?"

"I was there! She didn't attack them. They're lying." He remembered Mrs Weerasinghe's cold stare in Karadi's direction the previous day. This must be her plan!

"I have *no idea* what you're talking about! Tell me what on earth has been going on."

He quickly recounted what had happened with the

key, and Karadi, and his journey so far, and Sani's expression grew outraged and scared by turn as he spoke.

"You can't be serious!" she said. "We need to go back home right now."

"No. I'm in too deep. Once the Weerasinghes have the key they'll report me as a thief, and I have no proof they did it to clear my name. My parents will be shamed and the whole family disgraced. They're just waiting till they get the key so no one else will look for it."

"So where's the key now?" said Sani.

Nuwan smiled without humour. "You know what, you're not going to believe it…"

Chapter Seventeen

"This is *nuts*," said Sani. "You are nuts."

"You had to be there! It made perfect sense at the time."

"Absolute nuts!"

Nuwan sighed. "How did you find me anyway?"

"Well, it wasn't easy. I was looking for half a day. Then I found this." She pointed to his hand-drawn map. "I'd recognise your terrible drawings anywhere."

"It's a good route, though, you have to admit. I just need to get a move on."

"I'm glad I caught you before you

headed into the forest or I'd have never found you."
Sani picked up her heavy bag and hoisted it on her
shoulders. "What now?"

"OK, so I have a plan. It involves the bear."

Sani closed her eyes and sighed. "Do I even want
to ask?"

"Probably not. Stay here, I'll be right back."

Karadi was outside the cave this time as Nuwan
walked up through the sun-baked ground. Here and
there were deep cracks in the parched soil.

He didn't want to sneak up and surprise Karadi.
Nor did he think it was a great idea to go in making a
huge noise. He just wanted her to know he was coming
and not see him as a threat or a nuisance.

She looked at him, and he could swear she seemed
to sigh and roll her eyes, as if she was saying, *Oh here
we go again.*

She grunted. She sounded annoyed. But at least it
wasn't a roar like before.

"We need to get moving," he said to Karadi softly.
"For both our sakes."

He took a step closer, his eyes on her claws.

She looked at him warily. But she didn't move.

He wiped some sweat off his brow and took another

tiny step forward. "Thank you for not trying to kill me."

Karadi snuffled at the ground, as if she was looking for something.

That reminded Nuwan of what he had to do. He was close enough.

He took off his bag slowly, keeping his gaze on Karadi. She looked up at the movement. He took out the books, transferring them to the crook of his left arm. Then he took out a small sapodilla and offered it to the bear.

Karadi looked at him, and then at his hand. Her expression changed at once, to one of great interest.

Nuwan held his breath, holding out the fruit steadily. "Hello, Karadi. This is for you."

She shuffled towards him. Nuwan's breathing grew fast as the grunting ball of fluff moved closer. Karadi's breathing was ragged. Was she nervous too?

Even as he willed himself not to, his eyes went to her claws. Every fibre of his being was telling him to turn around and run away. But it was too late now anyway. And, also, he didn't want to leave.

She came right up to him and nipped at the sapodilla in his hand, knocking it to the ground. She snuffled and clawed at it, breaking it into little bits.

She then seemed to suck them in through her mouth, making a great racket of smacking noises as she ate.

Nuwan stayed there silently until she'd finished. He put the books back carefully into the bag.

She sat back and looked up at him. The key swung about on her chest.

He looked at it with dread. What if she dropped it somewhere? Or ripped it off from around her neck? Or he couldn't find her again? So many things could go wrong with this plan of his. Maybe Sani was right and it was completely nuts.

"Let's go," he said softly. He turned and walked away. He stopped after a few steps to turn around. Karadi was still sitting there, looking at him.

"Come on, Karadi," he said. "I've got more lovely sapodilla if you want?" He didn't want to seem too demanding, just inviting, so he turned back and continued on. *Please please please*, he thought. *I couldn't bear it if something bad happened to you because of me.*

A swish sounded behind him. Hardly daring to hope, he sneaked a peek over his shoulder. Karadi was moving slowly, following him at a distance.

Nuwan couldn't contain his excitement. It took everything to keep from whooping loudly. He walked on slowly, humming to himself. He had a bear behind him. *Behind him!* And Nuwan was leading them both to safety. Their journey had begun!

Chapter Eighteen

Sani was waiting for him by a tamarind tree near the map.

"Where did you go?" she said. "You've been ages!"

Nuwan stopped and, with a small smile on his face, looked behind him to where Karadi was approaching.

Sani squealed. Nuwan made a face at her. *Don't*, he mouthed.

Karadi had stopped too, and she watched the children carefully from a distance. Sani looked as though she was pressing so hard against the tree that she'd come out the other side.

"Don't worry," Nuwan said softly. "She's been following me all the way here. She's not going to hurt me."

"That's not what I'm worried about!" she hissed. "I'm more worried that she'll hurt *me*."

"She can see we're together. She'll understand we're friends so you're a friend to her too."

"I don't think bears are known for their logical thinking. They just think 'HUMAN. KILL.'"

"Give her a chance," said Nuwan.

"I don't have any choice, do I?"

He shook his head. "Not really," he said, and the two friends stood there, waiting to see what the wild animal would do next.

"Come on," said Nuwan, eventually. "Let's get going."

"Where to?"

"The King's City. You're coming, aren't you?"

"What about..." Sani jerked her head towards Karadi. "Her?"

"She'll follow. Come on." He took Sani's arm and turned her away.

Sani turned back at once. "I am NOT turning my back on a bear!"

"Stop being silly. She trusts you."

"I don't care if she trusts me! I don't trust her!"

Nuwan was starting to get impatient. "We need to get moving. I have three and a half days to get to the King's City in time for the hand over of the key. I'm lucky it's a ceremonial procession and it's going very slowly and stopping all over the place. If you don't want to come with me, we can say goodbye now."

Sani narrowed her eyes at him. "Nuwan, I came to find you because I wanted to warn you and also give you some moral support when you were alone. But now I find you have the Key of Nissanka with you, two murderous villains on your back, and a ferocious *bear* as your new best friend."

"Put like that, I'm not surprised you want to go back," said Nuwan glumly, wretched at the idea of losing Sani so soon.

"Go back?" Sani laughed. "Not a chance! It's all going down round here!"

"You're such a good friend!" Nuwan chuckled and pulled her arm again. "Come on, no more arguments then."

Sani looked nervously at Karadi but allowed herself to be pulled away. She looked over her shoulder once or twice at the bear as they walked.

"She's not coming, you know."

"She will." Nuwan was confident of that. It had been the same earlier as well. She didn't like demands but seemed happy to come along if she felt like it.

Sure enough, after a few moments, Nuwan heard rustling behind them. She kept even further back than before but he figured she'd get comfortable with them soon.

They walked for about an hour before they stopped for lunch. Karadi watched as they settled on the ground. Nuwan had seen her stop at an anthill not long before so he reckoned she was probably all fed.

Sani took out some delicious-smelling food from her bag. "I brought some rice and curries. But…" she glanced at Karadi, "is it wise to eat this in front of a bear?"

"Sure!" said Nuwan, holding his hands out. "Give it here. She's not interested."

Sani handed a parcel to him and he tucked in at once, eating very fast. As he paused for breath, Karadi slunk away.

"Where's she going?" said Sani.

"Probably to rest," said Nuwan, going back to his food.

"Oh yes. They sleep during the day, don't they?

Since it's midday she probably feels sleepy."

Nuwan took a bite of some sweet dodol that Sani'd brought for afters. "We could continue when she's up from her nap and it's cooler. We can go on till it gets properly dark and then we'll eat again and stop for the night."

Sani nodded, her mouth full of dodol. They drank the water and leaned back against tree trunks. It was cool in the shady spot where they'd stopped, and soon Nuwan was nodding off too. He slipped into a deep, dreamless sleep for the next couple of hours.

When he opened his eyes again he was lying on his side on the ground, having slipped off the tree. Sani was snoring softly opposite him but Karadi was back. She sat by herself, still keeping her distance from Nuwan and Sani.

Nuwan shook Sani awake. "Let's go on," he said as she stretched and groaned. "We can get in a few more hours before we have to stop again."

She looked at Karadi, sitting there patiently. "Oh, she's back!"

Nuwan smiled. "I know. Good news, isn't it? When she left I was a bit worried that she'd gone off for good."

Sani stood up and rubbed sand off her legs and

arms. "I'm really glad she doesn't come any closer, though."

Nuwan looked over his shoulder as they started off. Karadi was pootling around but looked up curiously as the children walked off. She growled softly and followed them, bouncing on her paws. *I'm coming!* At least, Nuwan was pretty sure that's what she said.

"You sure you don't want to risk taking the North Road?" said Sani. She was still bleary after her nap. "It's so much quicker."

"I just don't trust the Weerasinghes. They'll still be looking for Karadi and the key – I want to stay as far out of their way as I can. And we need to watch out for the wildlife authorities who'll be looking for her too."

"Makes sense." Sani staggered past a fallen jack tree crawling with ants. "How do we get the key off Karadi when we get there?"

Nuwan turned to look at Karadi as they walked. "I don't know," he said honestly. "But when we get to the Queen and they see the key round her neck, they'll know that I'm not a thief and Karadi isn't a murderous beast. Then everything will be well again."

They came to the coast just as the sun was setting, darkening the day into a reddish glow. The forest became sparser as it got closer to the sea.

Sani had found a good spot for a camp and was already sitting down, pulling food out of her bag. "What about Karadi?" she said.

Nuwan turned back to see the bear standing at a distance as always. She seemed to nod her head at Nuwan and then ambled away into the trees.

"She's probably out looking for food." Nuwan sat down on the mat opposite Sani. "I think she just reassured me that she'll be back."

Sani laughed. "I hope you're right and she didn't just run off with the key."

Nuwan chuckled in reply. But he was secretly wondering that too…

He took up a chunk of dodol and bit into it.

"What a funny life." Sani took her own huge bite of dodol. "Sleeping most of the day and then up at night."

Nuwan licked the sweetness off his fingers. "Did you know that bears in some countries sleep for ages at a time. Like *months*."

"*What*? Months! How is that even possible?"

"I don't know. Apparently they don't need food and water." Nuwan shrugged. "Just sleep. My father told me about it."

"How strange. I'm glad Karadi isn't going to

go off and sleep for months!"

"Yeah, lucky for us that sloth bears don't do that."

Sani began rummaging around in her bag. "Bring me some branches for a fire."

Nuwan went off and found some branches. They were all twiggy and as dry as a bone, so it was an easy fire to light. Sani had brought matches and they had everything they needed to get it going.

The flames flared up around them, making them hotter than ever.

"Sorry," said Sani apologetically. "But we need to have a fire going all night so we're safe from any animals."

Nuwan nodded in agreement. "It's good! I'll sleep much better now."

Sani lay back down on a mat after putting her bag to one side.

Nuwan continued to sit with his back against the tree for a while, listening to Sani's snores. What would his family be thinking now? Were they furious? Frightened? Sad? He couldn't bear any of it. But the one emotion he was sure they were feeling was the most upsetting for him.

Disappointment.

Chapter Nineteen

When Nuwan woke up the next morning, Karadi was still missing. The fire had died out and the day was hotting up early, though Sani was still sleeping soundly.

He made his way to the sea and washed himself. Far out at sea he saw the misty plume of air from a whale in the water. The sight made him smile. It was a good start to the day.

When he got back, Sani was awake and folding up the mat. Karadi had returned, and Sani was eyeing her warily as she pushed the mat into her bag.

"Oh, you've been in the sea!" She thrust her bag at Nuwan and ran off, her figure getting smaller as it went down the beach between mudilla trees.

"Hey, Karadi!" Nuwan called out as he bent down to retrieve his bag. "I hope you had a good night of, er, whatever it is you do." She had probably been out roaming the place and hunting for termites, or whatever horrors she ate.

The bear ignored him and pottered around, nosing between stones and under bushes.

When Sani came back, they were ready to leave. "We should get to the port by midday if we walk fast." Nuwan threw her bag to her, and she caught it with a thump.

"Sounds perfect." She slung it over her back and turned to go. "Karadi will be eager for her nap by then."

"Let's keep close to the coast but stay within the trees. We won't be seen then and Karadi will be more comfortable too."

"Good idea!" Sani jumped on a rock, running over it and then down. "We don't want to scare people to death if they come across a bear."

Nuwan turned to look at Karadi, who was taking Sani's exact path over the rocks. At the end she launched herself to the ground with a bump, the key swinging wildly on her neck. "I wish the white mark on her leg wasn't so visible. That way she could be any old bear and not so easily recognisable."

He felt so responsible for her safety. He couldn't let any harm come to her.

Sani handed Nuwan a squashed rice cake. "Do you think we should take the key off her now, instead of taking her right to the King's City?" She frowned as she took a big bite of her rice cake, dropping crumbs on her dress. "Is it wrong to take her away from her territory to somewhere so unfamiliar? What about when we get close to all those humans?"

"I was thinking the same thing, actually," said Nuwan. "But…" His voice trailed away, unsure if he should say anything.

Sani looked at him closely. "Don't worry, I get it."

"It's not that I don't trust her," he said quickly. "It's just … she's a wild animal. I don't know how she'd react if I went that close."

"Let's see how it goes." Sani bit into a stick of sugar cane with a massive crunch. They were passing under a copse of sapodilla trees now. "She's not going to be best friends with us overnight. We should be careful not to spook her."

Karadi was making great grunting, snorting noises as she scoffed down the fallen sapodilla fruits from under the trees. Nuwan and Sani watched her, giving her the space and time to have her snack in peace.

"I'm really glad I'm not keen on sapodilla," said Sani. "Imagine fighting her for one of those." They giggled as they waited for her to finish.

When they looked back next, Karadi had finished and looked like she was waiting for them to move on.

"Come on, Karadi," called Nuwan. "Two and a half days left and we have plenty of walking to do. We're going to have to go really fast so we get to the port quickly."

But, as usual, she watched them for a bit before following. Nuwan was beginning to understand that she was making sure they were serious about moving on rather than just going about some random human activities.

They came upon the port quite suddenly. The forest started thinning, and they were forced to move inland a little. Through the gaps in the trees they could make out a large ship sailing out at sea. As they walked on, an air of busyness was suddenly everywhere. And they were really close to a road!

As they emerged from the trees and approached

the road, a boy came down it, whistling. He nodded at Nuwan and Sani as he approached. Then his eyes widened as he looked behind them and he whispered, "Bear!" before hurrying off very fast.

Sani grabbed Nuwan by the arm and started dragging him down the road after the boy. "We need to act scared!" she hissed.

Karadi had stopped and was looking confused. Which was probably for the best. They did not want her following them this time. "Wait here!" said Nuwan. "We'll be back!"

They caught up with the boy quickly. "Thanks for the warning," said Sani.

He nodded. "S'all right. Glad you got away."

"Is this the way to the port?" said Sani, feigning ignorance even though they could see it in front of them.

The boy pointed. "Yes! It's right there!"

"Great!" said Nuwan. "We're here to see our father. See you later."

The boy nodded and went on. Nuwan slowed down and whispered to Sani that they should dawdle for a short while before going back, in case the boy turned round.

Karadi was waiting patiently when they got back.

They walked away from the road a little and settled down on the ground for lunch and the bear bounded off at once, away to her nap.

"Do you think we could go to the port?" Sani was rooting around in her bag. "We might be able to find some food. We don't have much left."

"Can't see why not, actually." Nuwan gnawed at the end of a sugar cane and then spat it out. His stomach grumbled. "No one knows we're here."

They picked up their bags and got to their feet. A figure moved silkily through the trees up ahead. "Look, Sani," said Nuwan. "A leopard!"

The leopard turned at the sound of his voice. It was a really magnificent animal with a slightly torn ear.

"Looks a bit different from the leopards down our way," said Sani, as it sprinted off. "Very nice."

They walked down the road towards the port in the direction the boy had gone. The road got busier and busier as they headed towards the sea.

The beach was full of hustle and bustle. It reminded Nuwan of the market in their town. Several huge ships were in the water, their masts high and billowing in the wind.

Lines of men laboured in the hot sun, carrying heavy sacks to and from the ships. Merchants scurried about attending to their cargo. Everyone looked too busy for words.

Sani bought some chilli pineapple from a seller and gave a slice to Nuwan. They ate the sweet fruit with the juice running down their arms. The wind whipped wildly and coconut trees bent low to the sand.

"Look," said Nuwan. "Something's happening over there. Let's go see."

They made their way to where a knot of people were gathered. As they got closer, a couple standing in front of them turned sharply around. Nuwan jumped out of his skin, not able to help gasping in surprise. Sani's eyes goggled.

"Ah, Nuwan," said Mrs Weerasinghe. "Wonderful to meet you again!"

Chapter Twenty

"Looks like you've got yourself a friend," said Mr Weerasinghe, nodding at Sani. He was covered in several plasters and bandages from his fake bear attack. "What are you doing here?"

"Just visiting," said Nuwan, trying to act nonchalant.

"Same as you, no?" said Sani. "It's not against the law."

Nuwan nudged her with his foot. He wished she would shut up. He didn't want to antagonise the couple.

Mrs Weerasinghe looked as if she was

about to tell Sani off but then changed her mind. "We've been waiting for you. We knew you'd come here."

Nuwan's stomach churned.

"That's not true," said Sani. "How could you have known we'd be here?"

Mr Weerasinghe rolled his eyes. "You left us a very handy map."

Nuwan's heart sank to the pit of his stomach.

"At first we thought it was a trick," Mrs Weerasinghe smirked. "Surely nobody's that incompetent? But no, turns out you are. You might as well have sent us a letter inviting us."

"I don't know what you want from us but you're wasting your time," said Sani. "We've got nothing."

Mrs Weerasinghe smiled. "Then why didn't you two just go home?"

Nuwan tried not to despair. Whatever they did, this pair were always ahead of them. As if that wasn't bad enough, Mrs Weerasinghe's next words made his blood run cold.

"We have people looking for the bear, too, of course. That's the main thing. And they know to make sure the key comes to me once they get the beast."

"That's right," said Mr Weerasinghe.

Mrs Weerasinghe looked mildly irritated at this interjection from her husband. The crowd shifted and a boy pushed his way between the Weerasinghes and the children. He stopped when he saw Nuwan.

"Oh, I keep bumping into you!" He laughed. "Good there's no bear hanging about this time, eh?"

Nuwan's face burned with horror. He tried to shush the boy by laughing nervously, although that came out as a croak. Sani grabbed the boy by the arm, startling him.

"Haha," said Sani. "Come on, let's go see the big ship there." She began to drag him away as if they were best friends.

"Wait!" said Mrs Weerasinghe, authoritatively. Sani pretended not to hear but the boy stopped and turned to her in spite of Sani's efforts. "What did you say? *Good there's no bear?*"

"He's in a hurry!" said Nuwan, taking the boy's other arm and trying to steer him away.

"Hang on!" said the boy. He looked at Mrs Weerasinghe. "Yes, I said bear. There was a bear following these two when I saw them earlier."

"How *interesting*," said Mrs Weerasinghe. "What a happy coincidence. Where did you see this bear, boy?"

Nuwan felt nauseous with dread. Surely he wasn't

going to give Mrs Weerasinghe Karadi's location too?

But he was. "Somewhere close to the road. A few minutes from the port. Must have gone away now, though."

"Somehow, I doubt that." Mrs Weerasinghe smiled at him and said pointedly, "You can go now. I have a bit of unfinished business with these two."

The boy's smiled wavered, unsure of what was going on. He shrugged and disappeared into the crowd.

"I've tried to be patient with you," said Mrs Weerasinghe. "I don't know what you're playing at, but you're not going to win. The key is mine and I will get it off that blasted bear if it's the last thing I do." She looked thoughtfully at the children. "Oh, get off with you. You can go."

"Wh-what?" said Nuwan before he could stop himself. Sani was looking at the woman curiously, and Mr Weerasinghe made a slight gesture at his wife as if asking her what was going on.

"That's what I said. Run along then," she said shortly, turning away. She walked away primly, tucking her sari fall into her waistband.

"She didn't even waste time threatening us!" Nuwan stared in astonishment at Sani.

Sani watched them walk away. "They don't have

time to lose by bullying children. The ceremony is in three days. They need to find that key."

"Then we don't have time to lose, either. We need to get out of here. Get Karadi away."

Sani put a hand on his arm to stop him. "Hang on. What if they've got someone watching us? That boy told them we were with Karadi. The worst thing we can do now is lead them straight to her."

Nuwan suddenly felt tears prickle his eyes. "I can't believe we have to leave her alone for her own safety. But I'd never forgive myself if something happened to her."

Nuwan imagined Karadi fast asleep now in a den somewhere. She had no idea about any danger she was in. She was bright and curious, and so loyal.

"Me neither," said Sani quietly.

"I know," he said to Sani. "Let's pretend we're here for the day just to explore the port and slip away once it's dark."

They walked away down the beach, the wind billowing through their clothes. "Will Karadi be OK if we don't return soon?" asked Sani.

Nuwan had been wondering that. Would she be waiting for them? Confused about why they hadn't come back?

"I'm sure she'll be fine," he said, trying to reassure himself as much as Sani. "She's a wild animal. She'll probably go back home if she doesn't see us again."

The children looked at each other sadly.

They spent the afternoon wandering around the beach, watching the ships being loaded and unloaded, and generally getting in people's way. There was a carnival atmosphere about the place, but their hearts weren't in it. Nuwan spent the whole time agonising about Karadi, and he knew that Sani was doing the same.

They didn't come across the Weerasinghes again in spite of keeping an eye out for them, but they felt sure that eyes would be on them nonetheless. They sat on the beach watching the sunset as the hubbub around them died down. Gusts of wind blew sand in their eyes as the setting sun turned the water a liquid burnt orange.

"It's getting dark now. Let's split up and each join a family leaving the beach," whispered Sani. "That way it'll look like we're going back home with our folks."

"OK. And then we meet back where we left Karadi?"

Sani nodded and they stood up from the soft sand. A few people were milling about but the beach was emptying fast.

Nuwan licked the saltiness off his lips and joined a large family that were heading home. He fell into step with the grandmother, who was lagging slightly behind, and asked if he could carry her bag for her, which she gave him gratefully.

With the bag slung over his shoulder next to his own, he walked out easily with them, pretending in his head that he knew them. He saw Sani leave with a group of women and girls.

The family he was with began to get on to some waiting carts. Nuwan bustled about, helping the grandmother inside and looking like he belonged with them. He set her bag down in a spare bit of the cart with a smile. "There you go!" he said.

"Thank you!" called out a man and Nuwan stepped back quickly into a bunch of coconut trees as the cart started to move away. Anyone watching would think he'd left with his family.

It was cool and dark under the trees. He went as far back as possible, blending into the mass of twisting trunks. The sea had started to look mildly threatening in the dark, although the ships were lit up on the inside with lamps.

As far as he could tell no one was watching him. Even if they had been earlier, they would have gone away now, possibly following the family in the cart. Hopefully Sani had managed to get away too.

Nuwan set off to find Sani and Karadi as planned. He kept the road in sight but moved through the forest so he wouldn't be seen. There didn't seem to be much activity in the port now it was dark, but he didn't want to risk being seen anyway.

Something small was shuffling about near him. Taking care not to step on it, he moved on quickly, trying not to think about what it might be.

Even though he thought his eyes had adjusted well to the dark, he nearly fell over Sani sitting on a tree stump waiting for him. She hissed at him and steadied him before he fell.

"Ow," she said. And then, "Sit there. We're not exactly where we were earlier. I thought it was wiser to move a little."

He lowered himself next to her, careful not to kick her again. "Where's Karadi?" he whispered.

To his great relief Sani said, "She's over there, near that big tree."

Nuwan could make out the shape of a bear skulking about under the tree. She was making a sucking sound that made him shudder, but he felt like his heart was singing. Next to him he could see Sani beam in the dark.

Something large and prickly brushed against his leg, startling him into crying out loud.

"Shh!" said Sani. "Will you be quiet? We've lost any walking time today, maybe we should try to sleep now and leave very early in the morning?"

Nuwan tried to quiet his racing heart. "Didn't you see that ... that, *thing*?"

"Yes, it was a porcupine. Now go to sleep."

Nuwan felt sheepish as he settled down on his uncomfortable perch. It was like a party out here in the forest after dark. There seemed to be so many more creatures than the previous night. Sani hadn't taken out the sleeping mat this time but just passed him a sheet that he wrapped round himself, hoping he wouldn't be bitten by insects – or worse – by morning.

Nuwan was shaken awake by Sani the next morning at dawn. The light was just breaking and he could see where they were properly for the first time.

"Let's go!" Sani looked completely dishevelled and was sporting a massive insect bite on her arm. "Karadi's here. We'll wash on the way!"

Nuwan jumped up. "Coming!" he said, packing up hurriedly and going after her. Only two full days left and people were after them again. Karadi's life was in danger.

The bear trailed after them, though Nuwan realised that she was closer to them than she'd been before.

They walked very fast this time, hardly slowing to get out some food. Nuwan grabbed the last of the palmyra sprouts and crunched into them, sharing a few with Sani. Karadi bounded after them as they walked at top speed.

They walked for what felt like hours, keeping parallel to the road all the time. The sun burned down on them, frying their skin. Just when it felt as if Nuwan's side would burst from a stitch, he realised it was time to stop because Karadi was starting to slow down and her eyes had gone languid.

"Let's stop," he said to Sani. "Karadi's tired. She needs to rest."

"I do too, actually," said Sani, taking a huge gulp of water and making a long aaaaah sound of relief. Her hair was sleek with sweat. Nuwan realised he was the same as he dropped to the ground in exhaustion.

"I'm dead," said Nuwan. He crawled to the shade of some neem trees.

Karadi's expression changed from doleful to happy as soon as she saw they'd stopped.

"Did you see that!" said Nuwan. "She's happy! I saw it in her eyes."

Sani was smiling. "I saw that, actually. I think you're on to something."

"Of course I am. Everyone just sees a bear too. But if you stop to really look and observe you can see the feelings behind the scary exterior."

The sun was high in the sky as Karadi loped away, no doubt to find somewhere cosy to have her nap. They'd got used to the routine now, walking from early morning to lunchtime, stopping for Karadi's sleep during the brightest hours, and then continuing on till dusk.

Sani threw Nuwan a stick of peanut brittle as he settled back in the nook of a fallen tree. He crunched into it absently.

"Do you think we're going to make it?" he asked.

"Make what?" asked Sani. High above her a peacock stood on a woody stump of a branch, its sheaf of feathers trailing behind. But she was completely blind to its blue-green loveliness.

"I mean, do you think we'll succeed? We have such a big task ahead. Get to the palace ahead of the procession. Keep Karadi from being killed by the wildlife authorities and the Weerasinghes' 'people'.

We're already behind schedule!"

Sani looked at him carefully over her sugar cane. "Do you *want* to succeed?"

"Of course!"

"Then you have as good a chance as any." She shrugged.

"I really don't want to let my family down," he said in a small voice. "I MUST fix this. I can't let them be disgraced because of me."

Sani tapped her fingers along the top of the tree trunk behind her. "You want to prove something, so go prove it."

"I'm just thinking…" He wasn't sure what he was getting at himself. "It's just … I *always* mess up somehow, somewhere. I don't like to admit it, but Krish is right about that at least."

Sani looked at him scornfully. "So? Just because you don't get something right once, or twice, or a hundred times, that doesn't mean that's how it's always going to be. People make mistakes."

"You don't. Krish doesn't."

"I make plenty of mistakes." She stretched and had a drink of water. "So does Krish."

"No, he doesn't."

"What about that time you said he lost a book

crossing the river? It fell in and got washed away!"

"Ha! Yes that's true. I'd forgotten about that." He had to admit, he felt a thrill of delight thinking about it.

"Exactly!" said Sani.

"Exactly what?"

"You'd forgotten!" she said impatiently. "That's the point. It's not important. Even *you* didn't remember."

"Because it was a long time ago?"

"No. Because it's not important. Mistakes happen. That's how you learn."

Nuwan was stunned at what seemed like a great revelation. Krish wasn't always the perfect person he was now. Actually, he still wasn't perfect. He'd nearly set the house on fire recently.

Sani was leaning back against the tree with her head resting on her shoulder. She looked like she was nodding off.

But Nuwan's mind was whirring. Had *he* been putting Krish on a pedestal too?

Chapter Twenty-One

Nuwan dozed off shortly after, and when he woke up Sani had taken their bottles out of their bags. "I'm going to find us some water. I'll look for a village and a well."

"I'll come!" he said rubbing his eyes.

"No, stay here. What if Karadi comes back?"

She had a point. Nuwan sat up as she walked off with their bottles. The peacock was still there, sitting gracefully on the stick-like tree.

Hopefully Sani would get some food

from a kind villager too.

Nuwan whistled softly as he waited, watching hornbills wheeling in the sky. Everything seemed very calm – until he saw Sani coming back with a group of men carrying scary weapons.

Nuwan got up in alarm.

"See, I told you," Sani was saying to the men. "It's just me and my friend here. I don't know what you were expecting to find."

"What's going on?" said Nuwan.

"These people think that we know something about a bear."

"A hare?" said Nuwan, quick on the uptake.

"Oh, was it a hare?" said Sani, playing along and looking at the men innocently.

The men looked at them suspiciously. One of them with a red scarf answered. "No, a bear, as you very well know."

"We've not seen any bear, sir," said Nuwan. "We're just minding our own business, having a picnic."

"Where's the food?" asked red-scarf man.

"We, er… We finished already."

"Yeah, it was really nice," jumped in Sani.

"Hmm." The men didn't look convinced at all. The red-scarf man said to them sternly. "I hope you two aren't being silly and messing around."

"Us? No way. We're quite sensible."

"There are a few groups of us looking for the bear now. If you're stupid enough to be trying anything on, well, you'll get what you deserve from the bear." He shrugged and all three of them left the clearing.

Sani exhaled loudly. "Well, that was cheerful. What happened to not scaring children?"

"It's not funny!" The sight of all those weapons had terrified Nuwan. "There are so many of them! And they're all out there looking for Karadi!"

"Nuwan! Relax. We can't do anything right now. Karadi's probably asleep in a cave somewhere. *We* couldn't find her, let alone those galumphing crooks."

That made Nuwan feel a bit better. "Right, but as soon as she's back, we're out of here."

"Of course. Here." She passed him some food. "Eat something while we wait."

"I've realised something, Sani," said Nuwan, while they ate.

Sani looked up.

"I've put Karadi at so much risk already." He sighed. "I thought taking her to the King's City would clear both our names but it's just too dangerous. I'm going to have to take the key off her and let her go back to her home. Once I tell the Queen about the real thieves and how they've lied about the bear attack, she'll be left in peace."

Sani nodded and they both finished their food in silence. It was a long wait until evening fell and Karadi ambled back into the clearing.

"Karadi!" Relief flooded through Nuwan. He got up and went over to the bear, who was standing on all fours on the stump of a tree.

She looked up at Nuwan. Her eyes bored deep into him as she saw his serious expression.

"I'm sorry," he said. "There's something I have to do."

Karadi stared back at him, unblinking. Her eyes travelled to Sani, who was staying back and watching their conversation.

Nuwan came closer. "I have to say goodbye," he said gently. "I think it's time you went back to your home."

He moved his hands towards Karadi's neck. He'd never touched her before, and the thought made him nervous. The friendly happiness of earlier was gone from her eyes now. She looked at his hands coming towards her.

Karadi growled, making Nuwan jump back.

"Hey, Karadi, I'm not going to hurt you." He kept his voice gentle and pointed to the key round her neck. "I'm just taking that off you. OK?"

She said nothing but gazed at him mutinously. "OK, here goes," he whispered, and put his hands on the string.

Karadi lifted her head and roared, shocking Nuwan so much he fell back on to the ground.

"Nuwan!" cried Sani. "Get back here."

Karadi looked down at the boy on the ground. He should have been scared of her but he wasn't. He didn't believe she was angry. He'd learnt to read her enough to know that she was just sad.

He stretched out a hand placatingly. But she was having none of it and smacked it away. Nuwan felt a sting of pain and a tiny line of blood bloomed on his skin where he'd been scratched.

"What are you doing! Get away from her!" Sani's voice was high-pitched and panicked.

"No, hang on." Nuwan stayed in position and held up a hand to Sani. "Don't alarm her. She's not going to hurt me."

"She already *has*." Sani was sounding desperate. "Get away before she does anything worse."

Karadi looked down at him, and this time there was

a look of pleading in her eyes. He turned back to Sani. "It's not what you think. She's not going to hurt me. I *know* what she's trying to tell me."

"Well, get away from her first, whatever it is!"

Nuwan stood up. Looking Karadi firmly in the eye he backed away from her until he was standing next to Sani.

Sani sighed audibly. Karadi sat down on the tree stump and swivelled around, turning her back to them.

"We have a problem," said Nuwan.

"You don't say!" Sani rolled her eyes. "It's not safe for us to be here. She doesn't consider us friends any more – she might attack at any time."

"Sani, I told you, it's not what you think."

"Well, what is it then?"

Nuwan sighed, his eyes on Karadi's back. "We're still friends – that hasn't changed. She's just not willing to give up the key."

Chapter Twenty-Two

"A bear who won't give back a key!" Sani held her arms out and gestured in confusion. "This is ridiculous."

"I know, it would be funny if it wasn't such a disaster. But you saw her – she's serious about this."

"She's a *bear*. She's not going to be making any decisions for us! We've got to get the key back."

He raised an eyebrow. "Do you want to have a go?"

"Of course not."

Nuwan scratched his head. This was

perplexing.

"Do that thing you do, whatever it is," said Sani, "and work out what she's thinking."

He looked back at Karadi and her stiff body language. Clearly she was annoyed with them. And also frustrated. She wanted to protect the children. She also didn't want to hand over the key. Why?

"She's trusted us all this time," said Sani. "It's like she's been an equal partner in it all."

Nuwan turned over Sani's words in his head, thinking hard.

"I think you've got it," he said to Sani. "She *is* an equal partner. Or was. She knows we're on some kind of mission and we have enemies in the Weerasinghes who are after the key. But now we're dropping her and I don't think she likes that."

Sani looked startled. "That's right. She knew the writing was on the wall for her! That it was the end and she was going home."

"So she worked all that out from me trying to take back the key? Gosh, she's smarter than most humans I know."

Nuwan burst out laughing and, hearing it, Sani dissolved into fits of giggling too. Their chortling echoed around the clearing, making the peacock jump down from the tree in panic.

Karadi turned around. She climbed off the stump and took a few steps closer, intrigued by the laughing.

"You're very clever, aren't you?" Nuwan turned towards the bear and gazed at her admiringly. Her expression softened at his smile. She came a bit closer, and Nuwan's heart melted even more.

"OK, you were right," said Sani. "She doesn't look mad at all. I think all is forgiven."

Nuwan laughed. "Except she's probably saying, touch the key and I'll rip your arm off."

"Fair enough."

They lapsed into silence as the day darkened further into night.

"We'll get moving first thing in the morning," said Sani.

Nuwan nodded. "The ceremony is the day after tomorrow. We don't have much time to lose."

Sani wrapped herself in her sheet and curled up against a tree. After building a very small fire, Nuwan did the same opposite her. After a few moments, Karadi came and sat between the two of them. Nuwan smiled as he noticed they were like three points of a triangle.

Something suddenly occurred to him, something

that should have occurred to him long before now. "Sani, won't your parents be worried about you?"

She grinned at him across the soft smoke rising from the flames. "I wondered when you'd ask that."

"Sorry." He was mortified. "I've been so wrapped up in myself and all that's happened."

She waved a hand. "Don't worry about it."

Still, he felt ashamed. "So what happened? Did you explain where you were going?"

"I left a note that said you were going on a journey and I wanted to go with you."

"And they'll be OK with that?" Nuwan had to marvel at how easy it was for some people.

"Of course they won't! They'll be furious. But they couldn't stop me because I was too far away by the time they saw the note."

"You're a good friend," he said.

"So are you. You'd have done the same."

Nuwan wondered if that was true. Just last week he wouldn't have imagined he would ever be on a journey like this, with a bear at his side. Krish's delivery job completely paled into insignificance.

"You know something?" said Nuwan. "Everything happens for a reason. I've decided that when Karadi refused to give back the key just now, it was the best thing she could have done."

From opposite, Sani pulled the sheet closer around her. "How do you mean?"

"The wildlife authorities are already hunting for her. Whether we took the key or not, they're not going to leave her alone now. Even if the Weerasinghes are arrested, the authorities will want to be on the safe side and keep looking for Karadi. She'll still be in danger."

"That's true." Sani frowned. "So how can we keep her safe then? We can't look after her for ever."

"We have to prove to them somehow that she's not dangerous."

"But they've already seen the injuries on Mr Weerasinghe. They don't know he faked them."

An idea sparkled at the back of Nuwan's mind. "If there's *one* person who could pardon a bear, who do you think that would be?"

Sani thought for a minute. "The Queen?"

"Exactly!"

She held her palms up in confusion. "How, though?"

Nuwan was getting excited as the ideas were forming in his head. "Karadi didn't want to leave us because she was part of our team. So we have to treat her like that. We go with her to the King's City and tell the Queen about her part in saving the key as we hand it over. That will get her a pardon."

"I don't know," said Sani very slowly. "I really can't see how that could work. Taking a wild animal to meet the Queen. We don't know how Karadi would react. Imagine if she hurt someone. It'd be a disaster for her. We might as well hand her over directly to the wildlife authorities right now."

"I have *so much* faith that she wouldn't do anything of the sort. She's so loyal and so involved in this, I *know* she wants to do it herself."

"This whole plan. It seems like such a … *big* thing to accomplish."

"It is! But look at what we've achieved already." Nuwan's eyes shone in the dark as he reflected on how far they'd come. "If I had told you last week that we'd be going on a journey far away from home with an important historical artefact and accompanied by the fearsome Karadi, would you have thought *that* was possible?"

Sani chuckled. "No. I would have told you to get lost."

Nuwan laughed too. "See. We've done the unthinkable already."

Sani didn't say anything for a while after that, but

he could tell she was thinking hard. Karadi got up and started to make her way over some rocks off to the side of their camp. She'd probably go away to find food. But whatever she did now, she'd be back at their sides at dawn.

The fire was nearly out when Sani spoke again. "Why is this so important to you?"

"What do you mean? Why is what important?"

She gestured towards him and his bag lying on the ground next to him. "This. This journey, this mission, whatever you call it. Why was it so important for you to do it? It doesn't make any sense to me."

Nuwan shifted so he was looking away from her, in the direction Karadi had gone. He was silent for a long time before he answered. "I want my parents to be proud of me."

"Yes, you told me that, but of course they're proud of you. Why would you think otherwise?"

"Because, well, because I'm not like Krish, who's all reliable and responsible. They depend so much on him and never on me. I'm not even like Priya who's cute and tiny. I'm just … there."

"But you're so funny, and you get on with everyone and make friends everywhere you go."

"That's different." He felt a bit impatient that she

wasn't understanding. "I'm just not … useful."

Sani snorted with laughter, and then covered her mouth quickly. "Sorry," she said. "I know you're being serious, but you're not an ox cart or a coconut scraper or a garden digger, you're a person."

"But *Krish* is useful! He's been useful to them for a long time. Unlike me." He felt his eyes brimming and was glad of the darkness.

"People grow up in their own time. Also, your parents may have *needed* him to grow up quickly then. But things might have changed with you."

Nuwan turned that over in his mind. Sani did have a point there. When he was very little, Krish did loads more work and helped in the fields all day. He didn't have to any more as his parents' circumstances had changed, but he still enjoyed his delivery job and kept it for the money it gave him, and it fitted around his apprenticeship.

"I just wish they didn't compare me to him all the time," he said.

There was a silence. A cricket chirped.

"Do they, though?" said Sani quietly.

"Do they what?" he said. "Compare me to Krish? Of course they do." Nuwan tried to think of an example for her. He sifted through some incidences in his mind, discarding one after another as they wouldn't do.

The wind blew softly around them. The fire burned down until it was just a small smoulder on the ground.

"Actually, they don't," he said finally in a small voice. He couldn't believe he'd never seen this before. "The only person who compares me to him is *me*."

Chapter Twenty-Three

Nuwan woke up stiff and cramped and stretched his legs out painfully. It was still dark, but fingers of light were slowly appearing, reminding him that it was nearly morning.

He sat up with a jerk and woke Sani. "Let's go!" he said, seeing Karadi already waiting.

They packed up fast and moved off. Karadi seemed surprised but followed without fuss, bounding along behind them.

"It's not just the wildlife authorities

I'm worried about," said Sani, her eyes puffy with sleep. "Now that they've decided Karadi needs to be put to death, I'm worried that villagers will take it on themselves to do something if they see her."

"You're right," said Nuwan. "The sooner we get away from this area the—"

He stopped as Sani screamed. Nuwan turned back in alarm. The colour had drained out of her face and she continued to scream, startling Karadi and making her sway from side to side.

Nuwan ran to his friend. The ground she was standing on was all bloody. Sani looked like she was about to throw up with pain and terror. She'd stepped on a bear trap.

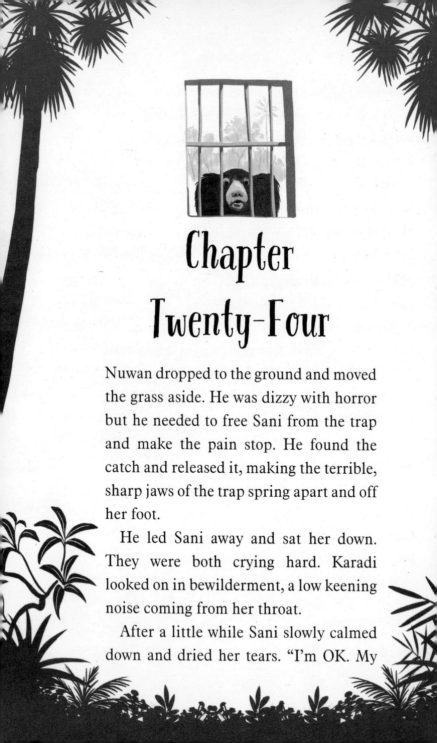

Chapter
Twenty-Four

Nuwan dropped to the ground and moved the grass aside. He was dizzy with horror but he needed to free Sani from the trap and make the pain stop. He found the catch and released it, making the terrible, sharp jaws of the trap spring apart and off her foot.

He led Sani away and sat her down. They were both crying hard. Karadi looked on in bewilderment, a low keening noise coming from her throat.

After a little while Sani slowly calmed down and dried her tears. "I'm OK. My foot hurts really badly, though."

"It looks bad," said Nuwan. The front of Sani's foot looked mangled and bloody, making him worried for her. "It needs to be seen to at once. Come on."

Sani didn't protest as he helped her up. With one arm over his shoulder she limped towards the road. He'd take her to a village for help.

"What about Karadi?" she whispered. "Could it … could it still hurt her?"

"No. It's fine." He called out to Karadi. "Stay here, we'll be back."

He felt sick with worry for Karadi too. Were there other traps? And if so, how many?

It was very slow progress and it felt like an age, but they eventually found a small village. As soon as they limped past the houses, people rushed up and took Sani to the medicine man.

Nuwan sat outside the medicine man's house while they attended to Sani. When they let him go in, he found his friend stretched out on a bed, her foot and lower leg encased in some kind of wrap.

Sani smiled at him. She looked much better, to his relief.

"She'll be fine," said the medicine man's assistant, Maliha, patting Nuwan's hand reassuringly.

"Where are your parents?"

"They're in the north," said Nuwan. "We were, er, making a journey."

The woman pursed her lips disapprovingly. "We'll send a message to them. She's going to be fine but she needs to stay off her feet for a week."

"A week!" exclaimed Nuwan and Sani.

"Yes. That's a nasty injury you have there."

"But we need to get going," said Nuwan.

"*You* can if you want to, but she's not going anywhere," said Maliha. "I don't know what you two are doing out in the forest anyway – don't you know there's an out-of-control bear on the loose?"

"A bear?" said Nuwan. Suddenly he stiffened.

"What's the matter?" said Maliha, looking from him to Sani. She was sitting bolt upright in bed now.

Behind Maliha was an open window. And through it poked a shaggy head with a long nose and two beady brown eyes.

Chapter Twenty-Five

"You should go," said Sani quickly, making eyes at Nuwan.

"Let me get you both something to drink first," said Maliha.

But before she could turn around, Nuwan jumped forward and gripped both her arms. "No! I mean … you're too kind. Just stay here." He tried to shoo Karadi away with his eyes without Maliha noticing.

She shrugged away from him, frowning. "It's no bother."

Luckily Karadi's head had disappeared

by the time Maliha turned round. She left the room and Nuwan ran to the window. Karadi was sitting under the window, looking up at him.

"What are you doing? Go!" He gestured at Karadi to leave. "I'll come back! But you have to leave right now."

"I'm all right, Karadi," said Sani from the bed. "Thank you for being so wonderful. Goodbye, little bear."

On hearing her voice, Karadi rose and looked at her mournfully through the window, then dropped down again and slunk away.

Nuwan sat on the side of Sani's bed, being careful of her injured leg.

"You should go," she told him.

"I can't, Sani. I don't know what I'll do without you. Maybe if I wait a day we could go together, slowly?"

"We don't have a day! It's tomorrow! Even now we've lost so much time and you'll never make it if you stay here any longer. This is where I say goodbye, Nuwan."

"Don't say that!"

Sani's eyes were misty. "I would have loved to see this through. But you can do this. What you need is some self-belief. Don't compare yourself to anyone.

You are you and you can do this."

Nuwan couldn't imagine going on without her. "You know what, I don't know if we can make it by tomorrow."

"Of course you will. Just go now and don't waste any time! The ceremony is in the evening, you can do this. You know it's important to you. I want you to do it, so you can prove, not to anybody else, but to *yourself* that you can."

"But I don't want to do it by myself!"

"You wanted to do it by yourself, and you *intended* to do it by yourself. Until I turned up."

He was silent. He could see in Sani's face how devastating it was for her to have to drop out.

"You go on," she said bravely. "Karadi will be waiting. My parents will come and pick me up."

Nuwan gave her a hug and left without looking back.

Chapter Twenty-Six

Nuwan and Karadi trudged away in the direction of the King's City. Instead of hanging back as she always did, Karadi stayed by Nuwan's side. They walked in silence, the pall of Sani's departure hanging over Nuwan all the way.

When it was time to stop, it was Karadi who took the lead. Nuwan was suddenly aware of her not being at his side. He stopped and looked back.

"What's the matter?"

She looked at him and Nuwan could swear one eyebrow was lifted slightly.

He realised with a start that it was the middle of the day. "Oh. Sorry. Yes, thanks for reminding me."

He picked a spot in the shade of a large ironwood tree. The forest seemed to be changing. The leaves were thicker, greener, the earth dark and compact.

Karadi came over and waited expectantly. Her face looked concerned, as if she were wondering if he'd be all right on his own.

"You go on." He waved her away. "I'll be fine."

Her head tilted slightly.

"Of course I'm sure. Go on, shoo."

Karadi ambled away. She seemed a bit curious about this slightly different forest and looked as if she was ready to explore. Nuwan smiled. At least she was enjoying herself.

He realised he hadn't eaten for ages and that Sani still had the food she'd got for them the previous day. He grimaced.

"I'm starving," he said aloud. He knew he'd have to stop feeling sorry for himself and get on with it now. He'd do what Sani had done and go to find a village where they might have some food. As Karadi had to rest, it wasn't wasted time anyway, though he was terrifyingly conscious of time passing now.

As they'd been walking parallel to the road the

whole time, he found it quite easily and followed it until he came to some sign of habitation. The trees were definitely thicker here, and there was a wetness in the air, even though it wasn't raining. He grew excited because he knew it meant they'd made good progress to the King's City. Where he was from, the land was arid, but the further south you went it changed dramatically until you came to rainforest.

He heard voices before he saw anything. There was the sound of small children playing, so he followed the noise and came to a fairly substantial village, with small paths and neat houses set here and there. The sandy paths were well swept and clean and a cow stood in a fenced area next to one of the houses. There was a well in the centre and he resolved to get some water as well. Three girls sat on the ground playing marbles, and a couple of people were walking down the path.

He stopped by the back of a house with a large mango tree outside, laden with fruit. A woman was standing there, hacking at a coconut. She looked up when she saw him.

"Do you need mangoes picked?" he asked.

"Yes!" She looked interested. "It's very high. Are you sure you can do it?"

Nuwan nodded. This was something he was actually good at!

The woman gave him a rope and basket, and Nuwan filled it with as many mangoes as he could, being careful to pick only the ripe ones as instructed. He lowered the basket down to the woman, and then lifted it again for more. He picked loads until his neck and arms ached and the woman had enough.

When he came back down the woman was beaming. "Take as many as you can carry. I have lots."

He stuffed them into his bag gratefully. It was a weirdly funny shape now, but he didn't mind at all. He pulled it over him and got ready to go.

"If you wait a bit longer, I can give you some more food," she said. "I'm in the middle of cooking."

The smell of cooking was irresistible and the idea of a proper meal was too tempting, so Nuwan accepted gratefully. He went back to the square and waited, taking out a mango and puncturing it, sucking the juicy orange flesh and sighing in contentment. He watched the girls with marbles and other villagers going about their business. When the food was ready, the woman came out and called him.

He sat in the kitchen with the woman and an older lady and they tucked in to the rice and curries. He thought of Sani's journey home and hoped she was OK too. Hopefully, she'd be picked up by a cart and leave with her parents. It wasn't as if she had anything to hide any more.

After they'd finished, Nuwan thanked them and was standing at their back door when he heard a commotion. Some people were running about. Nuwan managed to ask one what was going on.

"It's a bear," said the girl. "Some of the villagers have caught one."

"What?" Nuwan was struck by fear.

"You know! A bear. They are shaggy and have four…"

Nuwan dropped his bag and sprinted to the road, where two people were hurrying back.

"Where is it?" he asked them. "Where's the bear?

"Out of the way!" shouted someone else. It was all a bit chaotic. Nuwan looked up the road and his heart froze.

Karadi was hobbling down the road accompanied by a group of men. They had a rope around her neck with smaller ropes extending off it, and men were holding these, keeping as far away from her as possible.

Karadi was whimpering, pulling at the rope around her neck and then stopping as it tightened around her. She was in so much distress that it broke Nuwan's heart. He raced right up to her but she didn't seem to see him, and the men yelled in anger. One jerked him away by the back of his shirt.

"*What are you doing?*" he yelled at Nuwan. "Stand back!"

"Let her go!" shouted Nuwan, but no one took any notice of him.

A woman in the crowd shrieked and pointed. "Look at its leg!"

Dozens of pairs of eyes travelled to the tell-tale white on Karadi's leg. A whisper started.

What, really?

That one?

Karadi saw Nuwan then and yowled, a sound that cut deep into him. Her gaze locked on to his and looked at him pleadingly.

"What's that key?" said one of the men holding the ropes and squinting at Karadi as she thrashed about.

Nuwan didn't wait to see any more and grabbed the rope off him. He gripped it hard and kicked at the man, who let go in shock.

"What—?"

There was a yell as someone else let go of their rope, and people began to scream. Nuwan loosened his rope so that Karadi wouldn't get even more hurt than she already was, and she bared her teeth and roared.

The people around her scattered, letting go of the ropes and running for their lives. A few screamed and children cried as they ran away.

"Let's go," said Nuwan to Karadi, sprinting off into the trees. Karadi dropped on to her paws and ran after him. They thumped into the forest, the bear surprisingly fast as they thrashed through pathless shrubbery without looking back.

Nuwan slowed down when they came to a small stream. He couldn't bear to run any more. He was fully winded, having sprinted at speed all the way. Karadi showed no sign of fatigue but slowed down when she saw that he needed to stop. Nuwan knelt down on the ground and held his hands out to her.

She came close to him, whimpering slightly as she did so. A few pieces of rope trailed from her body on to the ground. She put her head down and lay in front of him on her stomach.

"Come here, you," Nuwan said gently. There were dribbles of blood on her neck and fur. He set to work unpicking the knots on the rope, careful not to rub against her wounds. She just lay there, flinching occasionally but not making a sound. It took him a long time to undo them all, but finally the ropes were in a pile by his side. He took her to the stream and washed the blood off carefully. Once he'd cleaned up the wounds, she lay back down and went to sleep, right there next to him.

It was only when she'd fallen asleep that Nuwan's tears started. Sniffing, he wiped them away and looked at the ground. He could have taken the key off Karadi when she was defenceless and he was tending to her wounds. He doubted she'd even notice. But it felt wrong. He'd never treat her like that.

He leaned back on the tree and then realised he'd left his bag at the village with everything in it.

Chapter Twenty-Seven

"I'll be back, I promise!" said Nuwan for the dozenth time that evening as Karadi nuzzled at him. Karadi had had a nice long nap but darkness had fallen and she'd become clingy after the earlier incident.

Nuwan couldn't blame her, but he had to go and get his bag back. He needed his water bottle for a start, or he'd never make it to his destination. And also, he was still determined to take the books as intended and hand them over to the monk safely. Just because he had bigger obstacles to overcome now, it didn't mean he'd forgotten the real reason he was here.

He squatted down and looked into Karadi's eyes. "Listen, I have to go and do this without you. It's much too risky for you to come. But I'll be back as fast as I can – we need to be somewhere tomorrow. Do you trust me?"

She looked back at him, eyes slightly watering. He wasn't sure how much she understood but she seemed to get the gist of it.

Yes, her eyes seemed to say to him. She sat back down.

"Good girl!" He stood up and moved away from her, trying to get his bearings. Because they'd run away so fast, he hadn't thought to keep close to the road, so he'd lost his sense of direction. No matter, he'd find his way back to Karadi. "Stay here, I won't be long."

He had a rough sense of which direction to go based on where the sun had set. He walked away in as much of a straight line as he could. He needed to follow the road to the village.

He felt like he'd been walking for a long time. Surely he should have come to the road by now? Just as his stomach was starting to tighten with nerves, he came right on to it.

The relief was huge. "Nearly there, Karadi," he said under his breath. "You stay put and I'll come back for you."

It was spooky, walking by himself at this time of night. Something flew past him and brushed his face with a velvety wing. It was an owl, which batted away silently into the trees. He shuddered and hurried on, his footsteps sounding loud.

He was glad of the road as he stumbled down it, looking for any sign of habitation at all. Something winked brightly in the dark on his left and he hurried on, hopeful that this was a sign that a village was coming up.

"Stay where you are, Karadi," he whispered to himself as he went. When he saw the first coconut-thatched roof he exhaled audibly. He recognised the village immediately.

The village was deathly quiet and he had no intention of calling attention to himself after what had happened earlier. He crept inside, seeing the same cow sitting down on the ground with its eyes closed. Nuwan wondered where the bag would be. Where was he when he heard about Karadi?

He was sure he was at the well but there was no sign of his bag there. He decided to check the woman's house where he'd eaten. He followed the path down to it in the dark. He went round to the back, as before. On the small bench that he was sitting at earlier was his bag. Someone had clearly brought it there for safekeeping. Even before he picked it up he got the fragrance of ripe mangoes. He smiled as he put the strap over his head.

He left the village briskly and without disturbing anyone. He ran up the road this time, eager to meet with Karadi again. He walked and walked, well into the night.

His heart soared when he came to the kaduru tree where he'd joined the road. But wait a minute, he thought. It looked all wrong. The ground looked burnt, as if it were to be used as a chena.

He hurried on and spotted the next kaduru tree soon after. But this wasn't right either.

Nuwan stopped and looked on both sides of the road. Even in the darkness he could see the place was full of kaduru trees.

"What—" He stopped dead in the middle of the road. He didn't remember seeing anything like this on the way to the village. But then he was just focused on finding it.

"I just need to keep going," he said. "I must have

missed it but that doesn't mean it wasn't there."

Something about the kaduru trees bothered him but he couldn't put his finger on what.

He went on, though his steps got more and more laboured the more he walked. He didn't recognise anything.

He stepped off the road and peered into the trees.

A wall of black shadows stared back at him.

He took a deep breath and steadied himself. "It's the darkness. I can't find my way back because of the darkness. I just need to wait and go back when it's light."

He sat right on the edge of the road, too terrified to go into the forest. He briefly wondered whether to light a fire now that he had his bag and possessions. But he decided against it and shut his eyes against the darkness.

He pictured Karadi still waiting by the ironwood tree, wondering why he was taking so long. He hoped she wasn't hungry.

His eyes snapped open. He'd remembered what was bothering him about the kaduru trees earlier. The fruit was poisonous. Even though he wasn't from the area, he knew not to eat it. Was it poisonous to bears?

Chapter Twenty-Eight

Nuwan woke up – he was being shaken violently like a rag. He gasped and sat up quickly.

"Hey boy, wake up!" said the man bending over him.

Nuwan looked around. He had fallen asleep by the side of the road and it was late morning. The man standing in front of him looked concerned. An ox cart was on the road, waiting patiently.

"Are you all right?" said the man.

"Y-yes. I'm fine."

"What are you doing here?"

"Sleeping."

The man rolled his eyes.

"Sorry, I'm just on a journey and stopped for the night."

"What! Here in this random spot in the middle of nowhere? Are you out of your mind? Where are your parents? Are you by yourself?"

Nuwan wasn't sure what to answer first so he just went with the last one. "No, I was with, er, someone. She's … around."

"An adult?"

"Yes." He was pretty sure Karadi was an adult. The man hadn't asked if she was an adult *human*.

The man frowned. "Are you in any sort of trouble?"

The question was such an understatement that Nuwan nearly burst out laughing. He shook his head. "My, er, friend will be here soon."

"I can give you a ride."

"Oh no! Don't worry at all, we're fine." He nodded firmly to demonstrate how under control everything was.

"Hmm. OK, then." The man still seemed unsure. "What about food? I have some I could spare."

"Actually," Nuwan patted his bag, "I have mangoes."

"That's all right then." He walked back to the cart

and got on. "I hope you get to your destination safely."

"So do I," Nuwan muttered.

The man got into the cart and drove off. "Thank you!" Nuwan called out. He was tired and slightly broken, and a cart ride home would have done him good. But he had to find Karadi. It was today. His head ached at the thought of the time he'd wasted last night.

His stomach was growling but Nuwan barely noticed as he got up and started walking. He walked down the road for five minutes. He had thought that when it was daylight, he'd come across something familiar from the previous day but it was still all so unfamiliar.

Another cart passed by, slowing down as it approached him. He ignored it and carried on. He came to an area full of kaduru trees again and stood there for a moment. The sun burned overhead.

He swayed on his feet and sat down quickly. He crawled to the shade and took deep breaths. He drank a huge gulp of water.

Opening his bag he took out a mango. To his surprise, among the mangoes there were several small parcels of food. No wonder his bag felt heavier than usual.

He opened up a parcel of roti and began to eat, grateful to the woman who'd done this. He gorged himself on the roti, and then the mangoes, eating fruit after fruit until he was so full he thought he might burst.

He sat there for about fifteen minutes, just thinking, and then got up. "OK, Karadi, here I come now. You'd better be waiting."

Slinging his bag across his chest, he went into the forest. Maybe this would be easier. He couldn't retrace his way via the road, so he'd go into the forest, once again keeping close to the road.

He set off feeling much lighter. "Karadi," he called out occasionally into the trees. He walked on, through forest that was getting increasingly thicker. At one point he stopped. Something had changed.

He looked around him. The trees were large, with trunks of substantial girth and leaves of the darkest, brightest greens. The undergrowth had thickened until everywhere was greenery or lush, wet earth.

He was in a rainforest.

"NO!" He turned around. He'd come too far. He was getting close to the King's City now, but that meant he'd left Karadi far behind. He started running then, back, back, back, feeling ruts and stones jab at his feet.

He felt pain and he knew he was bleeding from his soles, but he didn't care. Where was Karadi? What had he done? He'd left her by herself somewhere far behind and he couldn't find her now. She'd be wondering and wondering where he was.

Tears blurred his vision as he ran on aimlessly. He had no idea where he was, where the road was, what he was doing. He came to a small hillside and dropped down on to the ground. He was hot all over, but he felt cold inside. The ground was dry and sandy. His throat felt scratchy as if there was a huge lump inside.

He lay down on the ground and curled up. Why was it so cold? But the sun was shining brightly and he felt both cold and hot at the same time. He closed his eyes.

Nuwan didn't know how long he'd lain like that, but when he opened his eyes it was evening. All he could see was the ground in front of him. He tried to turn but his neck was stiff and his throat felt like sandpaper. His mouth was parched.

He sat up slowly, feeling like death. His head was heavy and his body felt weak, as if he wouldn't be able to walk a few steps. He opened the flap on his bag and took something out. A mango. How did it get in there? He bit into the skin, taking off a chunk and spat it out. Then he sucked the pulp and juice out of it. In one of the packages in the same bag were some rice cakes. He ate them all. He couldn't think – he sensed he was missing something. Was he supposed to be looking for someone? His brain felt slow and lethargic.

Where was he anyway? He had to get up. He had to be somewhere today, but where was it?

His body was burning up again. He fell back on the ground and floated off to sleep.

The next time he woke up he was still in the same place. He had no idea where he was or what he was doing. He wished his mother was there.

He was hungry again. Wasn't there some food by him earlier?

He looked around him for the bag but he couldn't find it. Maybe he'd been dreaming and there'd never been any food. There was a water bottle close by and he drank deeply from it, the water forming a river of coolness inside him.

"No, I did eat," he said aloud. He distinctly remembered the taste of sweet mangoes. He screwed up his face in concentration. He wasn't sure if he was imagining it, but he might even have picked them himself. From a very big tree.

He stood up slowly to look for the bag. It made him dizzy to walk. The bag was on the ground by a bush, looking like it'd been dragged there by an animal. The flap was open and there were tiny remains of mango and rice cakes, and various other things, on the ground around it. Something had come along, dragged the bag off and eaten whatever food it could take out.

Nuwan picked up the bag. One flap stayed closed – it was only the food the animals seemed to have wanted. He went back to where he'd been sitting and hugged the bag to himself. Somehow, without even looking, he knew that the contents of the bag were very precious and he had to look after them.

His body started to burn up again, and he whimpered for his mother. But he was alone in some sort of forest and nobody came to his aid. He began to hum a song and he felt himself grow sleepy.

Nuwan's eyes opened. Again, he had no idea how long he'd been sleeping. He felt he needed to be somewhere and it was of the utmost importance that he went there immediately. But his mind was woolly and he couldn't recall it. Hunger gnawed at his stomach. He was sleeping on a bag, and he remembered from earlier that there was no food in it. In a haze, he debated whether to go and search for something to eat. But his mind or body couldn't cope with that so he fell back into a fitful sleep.

He woke up again dying of hunger. Two small brown fruits were on the ground in front of him. His head hurt and he couldn't identify what they were but he picked the fruit up and ate them, peel and all. When he woke up again – it might have been minutes or hours later for all that he could tell – there were two more. Nuwan ate them up and fell back to sleep.

Chapter

Twenty-Nine

It was morning and sunlight fell on Nuwan's face. He frowned and put a hand over his eyes. He wanted to sleep a bit more.

Something was digging into him, and he realised the lump he was sleeping on was his bag. Still with his eyes closed, he pulled it out from underneath him and tossed it away.

For some reason Nuwan was drenched in sweat. He opened his eyes. In front of him on the ground were two small brown fruits, one of them slightly squashed.

Sapodilla. He sat up and took one, splitting it in half and eating it quickly as he realised how hungry he was. While he was eating the other, everything came flooding back.

"Karadi!" he said. He looked around him, and there she was.

She was sitting a little way from him, snuffling at something on the ground. She came bounding to him when she heard him call.

"You found me!" He smiled, though on some level it felt like crying. "I don't know how you did it, but thank you."

Karadi looked into his eyes, and in hers he saw only love and loyalty. She had looked for him when he didn't come back, and even though he didn't know it at the time, she'd been at his side and found him some food as well.

"You saved me," he whispered. "Something happened. I think I got a fever. I didn't know where I was, or what I was doing. But you found me, and now the fever's broken. How long was I asleep?"

Karadi's wounds from the villagers' ropes had healed. The key still hung round her neck, safer than ever.

"Come on," he said. "It's going to be a bit slow but

we're back on the road now. I don't know what day it is but we're going to continue on."

And with Karadi by his side, Nuwan started walking again, on the final leg of the journey to meet the Queen and save them both.

Chapter
Thirty

"All right, Karadi," said Nuwan as they walked along side by side, "this is what we're going to do."

Karadi glanced up at him out of the corner of her eye.

"So, first things first. However angry we are at someone, we don't scratch them, pinch them or maim them."

She grunted and looked the other way, as if she was saying, "Whatever."

"Don't you give me that attitude. This is important."

She didn't respond but he had the

distinct impression she was stamping her feet in annoyance as she walked.

Nuwan was starting to get tired and he knew it was time to stop because it was getting to the hottest part of the day. They were in the rainforest again, just as he'd been before when he was running aimlessly.

He heard the sound of water trickling and led the way to a small stream. "This is as good a place as any." He bent down and splashed water on his face. Karadi came next to him and drank water from the stream. In a while she waded in and lowered herself into the water, even though it was just knee-deep.

"That's right, I want a good wash too. But after my nap. I'm too tired now." From his bag he took out the sheet Sani had given him and sat himself down under a tree, wrapping the sheet around him. "Don't you go finding friends here and leaving me now."

Karadi remained flumped in the water as he drifted off to sleep.

Chapter
Thirty-One

Nuwan towelled himself off with the sheet and hung it to dry on a branch. Karadi was mooching about in the background, doing something terrible to what looked like an ants' nest. They'd start on their way now that Nuwan had rested and washed too.

He noticed pink blossoms on the top of a tree close by. The jungle was dense but Nuwan was determined to locate that tree in amongst all the others.

He finally did so and looked up. Jambu fruit! He climbed the tree quickly, careful to take his time finding a stable branch he could straddle. He picked a bunch of jambu and plucked one, crunching into its juicy pink flesh.

He must be close to habitation then, to see trees like this. He looked out over the canopy of trees into the distance and Nuwan nearly fell off the tree in astonishment. He hadn't realised that he was at the edge of the jungle and on the doorstep of what he was seeking

"Karadi, come here!" he called out.

Karadi came bounding up the tree. Nuwan moved over and Karadi sat next to him on the branch, both their legs swinging down as they looked ahead.

"Would you look at that?" Nuwan pointed.

A city spread out in the distance, with small villages beside it. In the middle of the city, next to a brilliant white temple, rose a great hill with a grand set of buildings right on the top. There were landscaped gardens and steps cut into the rock, as well as clear pools and paved walkways. A giant lion statue straddled the entrance to the stairway.

It was the royal palace.

They'd made it to the King's City. In spite of everything, they'd made it. Nuwan squeezed the sides of his head in excitement. He was finally here.

"Oh, Karadi, I can't believe it. The King's City!"

Karadi swung round the branch and dropped off to another branch, disappearing into the wilderness below.

"You don't know how significant this moment is!" Nuwan protested as he climbed down himself.

He found Karadi back at the ants' nest. "OK, you stay there. I'm going to go and check things out."

Karadi ignored him as she sucked up ants with a huge smacking noise. Nuwan shuddered and left her to it.

The jungle ended abruptly, and Nuwan burst out into the daylight. He stared upon the sight in front of him.

He was on the east side of the city and the royal complex. A river flowed nearby, over which a small bridge led to a paved road to the city and the palace. People walked about busily, no one so much as glancing in his direction.

He walked over the bridge and on to the paved road. A few elephants were bathing in the river and one was enjoying being scrubbed by his mahout. One side of the road was bounded by a white wall that was scalloped and cut through with various motifs.

As he got close to the entrance to the palace, the place got busier. Sellers pushing different carts, laden with everything from boiled chickpeas to woven sunhats, were going into the palace grounds. On the left were the grand gates to the city, standing open.

Was the parade over? Had the theft of the key been discovered already?

He decided to ask someone. He strolled over to a pineapple seller, wishing he had the money for the delicious-looking chunks of fruit. The old man had something like a box on two wheels, on the top of which was a shelf of pineapples. He slid a part of the shelf back, revealing that the space inside was full of even more fruit. He picked one up and began expertly cutting away the skin.

Nuwan cleared his throat. "Sorry, I was wondering what's happening here."

The old seller looked at him with mild amusement, still cutting. "Not from these parts, then?"

Nuwan shook his head. He wished the man would concentrate on the pineapple so that he didn't cut himself.

"There's a big parade happening today. The Queen is receiving something important."

"Today!" He tried to keep the excitement out of his

voice. "But I thought it was on Saturday."

"There was a delay on the way. One of the elephants started playing up and they had to send a replacement, so they lost a day."

Nuwan's relief knew no bounds. He said a silent prayer for the wayward elephant.

"Do we get to see it?" he asked.

"Of course! It's a nice day out. The grounds of the palace are open to the public for these events."

"So I could just ... walk in there?"

The old man frowned, looking a bit suspicious. He sliced through the body of the pineapple and fanned the pieces out. "Yes. As long as you're not planning any trouble!"

"Haha, of course not. Why would I?" The man was still looking a bit suspicious so, "Haha," Nuwan said again, for good measure.

The man slid the shelf back and shook some chilli salt over the pineapple.

"What time does it start?" Nuwan asked casually.

"In about an hour," said the old man. "If you want to see the Queen receive the parade that is. But the party itself will go on till late."

One hour! He had made it by the skin of his teeth.

"So, you'll be going then?" asked Nuwan.

"I wish. Business would have been good but I'm an old man – I'm tired already. I'll be heading off home as soon as I've sold this batch."

He thanked the man quickly and walked off again, blending into the crowds.

He had to go and get Karadi! They'd have to be in position and ready to reveal the key as soon as the theft was discovered.

He ran back through the crowd towards the bridge, annoying a few people as he accidentally jostled them, but he ran on without stopping.

Then a pair of hands grabbed him and pulled him aside. He struggled and tried to get free even as more people pushed past. "Sorry," he said. "I'm in a hurr—"

A cold chill went through Nuwan as he looked up and saw who'd grabbed him. Mr Weerasinghe held on with an iron grip while Mrs Weerasinghe glared at him.

"We knew it!" said Mr Weerasinghe. "We knew you'd be here, you little do-gooder!"

"Take him aside." Mrs Weerasinghe was very calm even as her eyes sparkled dangerously. "We're attracting a bit of attention here."

A few people had stopped to look as Nuwan struggled against the couple.

"Come on!" said Mr Weerasinghe. "Insolent boy," he said to a bystander.

"I don't have what you want!" said Nuwan. "You're wasting your time."

But Mr Weerasinghe dragged him off, his wife leading the way. "Oh, we're not making the mistake of letting you out of our sight again," he said.

Nuwan stopped struggling. He wasn't sure what the Weerasinghes wanted with him but he'd have to trick them if he wanted to get away. He acted like he'd given up and went with them without any resistance. Despite all the trouble they'd caused him, he was glad they were there. He had plans for them!

"Well, I'm glad you've decided to wise up," said Mr Weerasinghe.

Mr Weerasinghe held on to Nuwan's arm while they walked. They were taking him into the city. As soon as it looked like Mr Weerasinghe had relaxed, Nuwan jerked his arm away sharply and took off.

Mr Weerasinghe yelled and came after him, but Nuwan was free and he bolted into the crowd and was lost to sight.

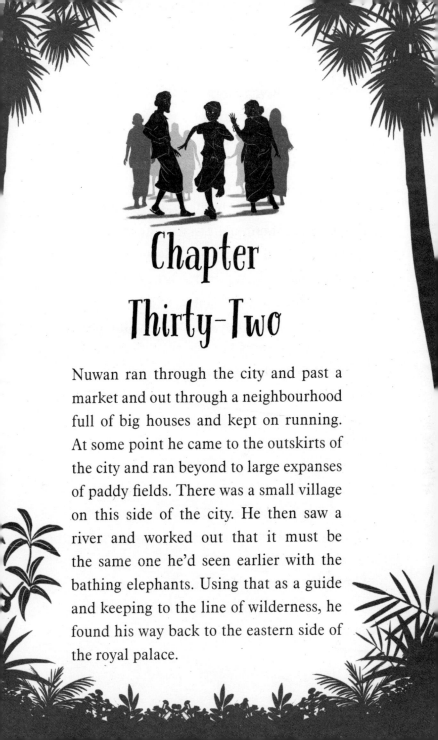

Chapter Thirty-Two

Nuwan ran through the city and past a market and out through a neighbourhood full of big houses and kept on running. At some point he came to the outskirts of the city and ran beyond to large expanses of paddy fields. There was a small village on this side of the city. He then saw a river and worked out that it must be the same one he'd seen earlier with the bathing elephants. Using that as a guide and keeping to the line of wilderness, he found his way back to the eastern side of the royal palace.

He slipped into the jungle and headed to where he'd left Karadi. She was sitting by the side of the stream trying to catch something. She looked up when she heard him and came bounding towards him.

"OK, Karadi, it's time!"

The key glimmered in the light as Karadi came towards him, her fur sticking up at all angles after being in the water. She stopped and looked at him as if awaiting her cue.

"Wait, we can't just march into the city together." He felt a stab of annoyance at the thought of the Weerasinghes.

"Actually, we can't march in there anyway, Weerasinghes or not."

Karadi inclined her head as if to ask why not.

"Come on!" he said. "You're a bear!"

That made him giggle, but he stopped quite soon when he realised he needed a plan. And quickly. There was no Sani to confer with any more. It was up to him to see this through. He was so nearly there now. He could do it.

Should he take the key with him and leave Karadi here? No, she had to be there for his plan to work. Besides, they'd done all this together and they'd finish this together.

They heard the sound of music striking up. He had to hurry!

But how could he take Karadi into the city without everyone scattering and screaming in fear?

A sudden, crazy idea came to him. But would it work?

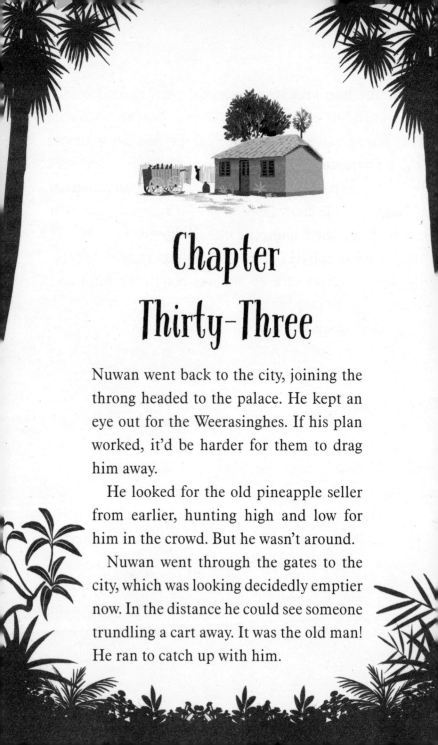

Chapter
Thirty-Three

Nuwan went back to the city, joining the throng headed to the palace. He kept an eye out for the Weerasinghes. If his plan worked, it'd be harder for them to drag him away.

He looked for the old pineapple seller from earlier, hunting high and low for him in the crowd. But he wasn't around.

Nuwan went through the gates to the city, which was looking decidedly emptier now. In the distance he could see someone trundling a cart away. It was the old man! He ran to catch up with him.

The man went slowly out of the city and down into one of the surrounding villages. Nuwan followed, keeping just out of sight.

The man opened a small wooden gate and went into the backyard of a house with the cart. After a moment the clattering sound of it stopped, as if he'd parked it there and gone into the house.

Nuwan stayed out of sight, lounging near a fence. When he was sure no one was about, he went and opened the gate carefully.

He knew he was doing a terrible thing, stealing the cart. But he'd think about how to make it up to the man somehow.

He tiptoed inside and round to the back. The cart was parked near the closed back door. Nuwan gripped the handles and pushed.

It made a clattering noise as it started up. Nuwan panicked and pushed harder, pushing with all his might and navigating it out through the gate. He picked up the pace, resulting in an even bigger clattering as he barrelled his way up the path and out of the village. He thought he heard a yell behind him but he wasn't sure – his heart was hammering so hard that he wasn't sure what was the cart and what was him.

He was creating a huge racket as he made his way to Karadi, and the cart was becoming increasingly difficult to push. He left it where it was and hurried to get the bear instead. She was where he'd left her, waiting expectantly. Nuwan ran to get the bag and threw it over his shoulder.

"Come on!" he said. "We've got to go NOW."

Karadi came bounding up as Nuwan went to the cart. He carefully lifted off the shelf from the top and set it on the ground. It was empty of pineapple chunks but still had a couple of knives and the chilli salt mixture. Nuwan looked inside the cart. The box was full of pineapples.

"Um, how do I do this now?"

He put one of the pineapples on the ground, whereupon Karadi immediately started clawing at it.

"Oh, stop that! Now is not the time for snacks. Hang on."

Nuwan removed the rest of the pineapples, then slid out the inner wooden casing and put it on the ground. Now the cart was just the sides and wheels, with no bottom. "Get in," he said.

Karadi stared back at him in confusion.

"You heard me right. In there." Nuwan pointed.

Karadi climbed over the edge of the cart as Nuwan

held it still. She dropped herself into the cart, her head popping comically out of the top as she peered over the sides.

"Down!" he said.

Nuwan fitted the shelf back over her. She was fully covered now, but she could walk along with the cart and breathe freely and see a little too. "You know, this just might work!"

But the pineapple cart didn't look very convincing empty like that.

"Hang on," he said, as he quickly started cutting up a pineapple. He chopped the top and tail off and cut off the skin as fast as he could. His chunks didn't look as neat as the seller's but it'd have to do. He quickly cut a couple more to fill up the tray. Through thin slits he could see Karadi inside the cart.

"OK, I think we're ready to go," he said. If you looked carefully, Karadi's paws were visible under the sides of the cart. But hopefully nobody would be looking!

He got back on to the road to the palace again, getting lost in the scrum of people. That number of people so close together meant that Karadi's legs weren't visible. A few times Nuwan thought he might have heard Karadi grunt, but thankfully the noise of the crowd drowned it out. Every so often he bent down and spoke a word of encouragement to her.

She was fine. This was it. They were going in.

As he reached the entrance to the palace, he noticed the temple next to it. It glistened a beautiful white and had a front yard with a peepul tree. Had he got time for this? But it was why he'd wanted to make the journey in the first place, after all.

He pushed the cart towards the temple. It was very empty, with no one about. Then he found he couldn't get the cart up the two wide steps leading to the entrance.

A monk passed by and stopped as he noticed Nuwan. "Are you looking for someone?"

"Yes," said Nuwan. He felt a stab of great pride. "I'm looking for the monk, Mahanama. I have some books for him."

"I will get the master." The man went off.

Nuwan stood there excitedly. He tapped the side of the cart to reassure Karadi he was still there. Karadi whimpered contentedly in response.

In a moment there was a shuffling and a very old monk in saffron robes came out. "Krishnan?" he said as he came over, then stopped and peered closely at Nuwan.

"No, master. I'm Krishnan's brother. He wasn't well so I brought your books this time."

He handed over the books to Mahanama. He had wondered whether to leave out the poetry book but then decided to hand it over anyway. If all went well, Mahanama would hear about what happened on the way to his books being delivered. And it would be safe with him if it was needed as evidence.

"Thank you. I thought I saw a resemblance." Mahanama handed over a coin to Nuwan.

Nuwan took it in shock. He had forgotten that he'd get paid for the delivery. "Thank you. I appreciate it."

He turned the cart to walk away, at which point Mahanama's gaze dropped to the wheels. Nuwan's heart skipped a beat as Mahanama raised his eyebrows at the sight of Karadi's shaggy black legs and curving claws.

Nuwan thought frantically for an explanation. "I… That… Er. So, um, I can explain."

But Mahanama held up his hand. "No need, son. I must admit a mild curiosity, but it doesn't look like you're ready to say. Stay safe." And he went back into the temple.

Nuwan was full of astonishment. As he wheeled the cart away he thought excitedly about what he could buy himself. But then he realised that he would have to give the coin to the old pineapple seller.

He whispered to Karadi as they rolled in through the palace gates. "OK, Karadi, this is our moment."

Chapter Thirty-Four

The palace gardens were huge and beautifully kept. Guards directed people in, past the formal gardens to a large lawn at the base of the mountaintop palace.

Nuwan pushed his pineapple cart, hoping no one would ask to buy any. The cart gave him a clear purpose for being there. If the Weerasinghes were to turn up, they'd find it more difficult to drag him away too.

On one side of the promenade, food stalls were set up. He wondered why anyone would buy anything from him when there was so much free food, but never mind. Karadi thumped against the cart a few times as if to remind him of her presence.

"Not yet," he hissed. "I need you to stay hidden for the moment."

The guards started shooing people aside, and Nuwan moved to the edge along with the others. He was content to be at the back, not making eye contact with anyone.

The promenade was now cleared for the parade of elephants, with onlookers crammed together closely on both sides.

And then the elephants walked in, their slow majestic gait keeping time with the flautists and drummers walking behind them. On the biggest elephant of all, who was walking behind two smaller ones, was the silver box containing the Key of Nissanka.

Nuwan's eyes were fixed on top of the elephant, his heart hammering as hard as the drumbeats around him.

He craned his neck over the heads in front to see the end of the promenade. He'd just noticed the dais where the Queen was sitting. On either side stood a selection of her lords. She was smaller than he'd expected and had a look of happy curiosity as the parade approached her.

On the other side, Nuwan caught a glimpse of Mrs Weerasinghe in the crowd. Her eyes widened as she saw him, and she whispered something to her husband next to her. In a flash they'd disappeared. Nuwan couldn't spot them again anywhere, but he knew they'd be making their way towards him.

The drummers increased the tempo and swarmed past the elephants to the front of the parade, followed by the flutes and cymbals. From the front, fire dancers joined them, twirling fireballs that lit up the evening.

Nuwan tried to move so the Weerasinghes wouldn't find him, but he was hemmed in tightly among the crowd with his cart.

The dancers whirled away from the parade and the music gradually stopped, ending with a single drumbeat, and then the musicians stepped away too.

In the silence the Queen stood up. She came down the dais towards the elephants. Two of the lords accompanied her, one step behind her on either side.

Nuwan was sick with fear. He glanced down into the cart and saw the glint of the key round Karadi's neck. What was he thinking? He couldn't just just jump out and offer the key, could he? To the Queen?

In front of all these people?

The head elephant, Ananda, knelt down. The hushed crowd watched in fascination as two mahouts removed the box from the cage-like structure on the elephant's back.

They handed it to the Queen, bowing deeply.

Nuwan's heart was bludgeoning at his chest. His hands had gone cold and stiff. He had to say something, *now.*

One of the lords took the casket from the Queen. Turning it to face her, he opened it.

Nuwan was faint with terror.

The Queen picked up the key from the box. She smiled, turning it over in her hands and a cheer went through the crowd. She seemed to pause for a second, and her glance slid back to the man who'd opened the box. She said something to him quietly. The other lord behind her stepped up, and his face blanched at whatever she'd said.

A whisper went through the crowd. *What's happening? Why isn't she taking it?* People began looking about for something else to happen.

The Queen was having a quick exchange in lowered voices with the men. The crowd grew confused.

Nuwan tried to move but his feet had turned to lead.

Had the Queen realised the key was a fake already?

"Is there a problem?" yelled someone in the crowd and a laugh went through the audience. The Queen looked up and smiled, though her face looked strained.

A hand fell on each of Nuwan's arms and the Weerasinghes gripped him hard. They pulled him with them and a few people groaned at being pushed aside.

He had to act now! Nuwan took a deep breath and called out. "Here!" He struggled against Mr and Mrs Weerasinghe, who clamped down even harder. "I have the key. The real one!"

There were a few giggles and people moved around to let him come forward. He rolled the cart in front of him with his foot and struggled through the crowd, bringing the reluctant Weerasinghes with him. A surprised guard tried to stop them, but Nuwan called out even louder. "Your Majes—"

The guard pushed him back angrily, but the Queen had seen him.

She turned in surprise. "What does the boy want? Let him speak."

Mr and Mrs Weerasinghe dropped their hold on him and melted back, pushing themselves into the now annoyed crowd.

"No, stay!" said Nuwan boldly. "I'm sure Her Majesty would want you to hear what I have to say about the key."

The guard stood behind the Weerasinghes now, blocking their way. Mrs Weerasinghe glared furiously at Nuwan, and Mr Weerasinghe looked back and forth shiftily as if working out how to escape.

"What's going on?" called out the Queen. "Did you say something about the key?" The crowd was completely silent now.

Someone screamed and pointed to the bottom of the cart, where Karadi's legs were visible, the white patch clearly showing too.

Nuwan gulped. They'd seen Karadi already. It was too early! He needed to explain everything first.

"Yes, Your Majesty. The Key of Nissanka."

The lords behind the Queen looked stunned. They looked at each other, and at the Queen, as if wondering whether to stop this spectacle right there or not.

Nuwan wheeled the cart slowly towards the Queen.

The entire lawn was silent except for the sound of the cart moving. Even the elephants seemed to have stopped their swaying. The smell of fire from the dancers earlier hung in the air. All eyes were fixed on Nuwan, and the pair of woolly legs visible at the bottom of the cart.

"Your Majesty," said Nuwan. He wasn't sure what to do so he bent low.

The Queen inclined her head. "What's your name?"

"Nuwan."

"Well, Nuwan. We're rather interested in what you have in your cart. I gather it's not just pineapples?"

There was some nervous laughter rippling through the crowd. Nobody liked the idea of what might be in there.

"No, madam," he said.

"Was there something you wanted to say?"

"Yes. I, um," he gulped. "I have the Key of Nissanka for you."

A stunned silence followed, but the Queen recovered quickly. "Is that so?"

"It's a long story, but someone tried to steal it. I accidentally took it away from them. They put a fake key in the box."

"What kind of nonsense is this, boy?" said one of the lords next to her.

The Queen frowned. "Let him finish."

"Er, so. Like I said, I accidentally took it away, and the thieves kept following me as I travelled all this way to bring it to you."

"Where have you come from?" asked the Queen.

"From the Great Library of the North," said Nuwan.

The Queen nodded slightly, looking impressed. "So you've had the key the entire way?"

"Yes, madam. I thought I should come and give it to you myself. But it wasn't actually me who brought it. Someone else guarded it all the way and never let it fall into any other hands. The key is only safe because of her."

"Who is it?" The Queen looked warily at the claws showing under the cart.

Nuwan took the shelf off the top of the cart and put it on the grass next to him. He peered inside and Karadi looked up at him a bit anxiously.

"It'll be all right," he whispered, and patted her paw. "Come on out."

And out climbed the bear. A gasp went around the crowd and there were a few screams as people scrambled to move away.

The guards drew their spears.

"No!" called out Nuwan. "She's not going to do anything."

"Is that…" The Queen shook her head. "Is that … a real bear?"

Nuwan turned to her pleadingly. "Yes, madam. Her name's Karadi. But she's not dangerous in any way."

"Sorry, I did wonder if it was a costume or something. So that's a real bear." The Queen glanced at the lords, who looked completely out of their depth.

"Please ask the guards not to come any closer," said Nuwan. "She's completely harmless unless someone bothers her."

Even though he meant that to be comforting, this seemed to alarm more people. Mothers picked up children and backed away. He noticed Mr and Mrs Weerasinghe shrink back too, but the guard's hands were firmly on them now.

The Queen gestured to the guards with a wave. They drew back their weapons. "What has this got to do with the key?" she asked.

"Look round her neck, Your Majesty," said Nuwan, pointing.

Another gasp went up from the crowd as they noticed the key nestled on Karadi's chest. The Queen's eyes grew very round, but Nuwan thought he detected a note of amusement in her expression too.

"So this is who guarded the key and helped you bring it here?"

"Yes, Your Majesty."

"Fair enough," said the Queen with a wry smile. "I can't imagine anyone messing with her."

"She would like to give it to you now," said Nuwan. He bent down and patted Karadi, whispering, "Go on, it's time to hand over the key."

"Don't be silly, boy!" said one of the lords as Karadi took a tentative step towards them. "Hold it off!"

The Queen looked tense, but she smiled at Nuwan. "It's been an extraordinary day, Lord Marasinghe. Maybe we should trust the boy and the bear."

Lord Marasinghe didn't look like he wanted to trust the boy, much less the bear. But he kept silent at the Queen's command.

"Come on," said Nuwan, and he walked ahead. As always, Karadi followed after a pause. The crowd watched in fascination.

Karadi walked slowly behind Nuwan on all fours. As she got closer, Nuwan could see the strain on the Queen's face. He stopped, touched the key and gestured for Karadi to approach the Queen.

Karadi padded slowly to the Queen. Nuwan could swear he heard the sharp inhalation from Lord Marasinghe as Karadi got closer. It seemed as if the whole crowd was holding their breath.

As soon as she got close to the Queen, one of the

guards drew out his spear sharply. Karadi looked at him for a moment, and then back to the Queen. The bear bowed her head.

Nuwan's heart was bursting with pride for Karadi. She'd kept calm and now was offering the key. The Queen looked to Nuwan and he nodded. She bent down and took the key off, lifting it over Karadi's head.

Karadi came loping back on all fours to Nuwan and he bent down and put his arms round her. He was overcome with emotion and burst into tears. The people around them whooped and clapped.

Nuwan straightened up and saw the Queen looking at him. She seemed moved by Karadi's actions too.

Lord Marasinghe was examining the key with a look of great delight on his face.

"Thank you," said the Queen. "We are much obliged to you and your bear, Nuwan. Could you tell us who stole the key and replaced it with the badly made fake one?"

Nuwan pointed to the Weerasinghes behind him. "The librarian and her husband."

All of prim Mrs Weerasinghe's composure deserted her completely as Lord Marasinghe made a small gesture and she and Mr Weerasinghe were swiftly removed by two guards.

And now for the really important part. Nuwan stood there for a minute and then said, "I shall take my leave shortly, madam, but there's one thing I must ask of you."

The Queen smiled at him. "Ask away. You've done something very brave and selfless, and I hope that there's something I can do for you."

Nuwan looked at Karadi. "Please call off the search for this bear, madam. The wildlife authorities want to put her down as they have been led to believe she's dangerous. But you've seen for yourself that she isn't."

"Of course," said the Queen. "Consider it done."

"Thank you," he said, blushing and bursting with happiness. Then he remembered something. "Oh, and one last thing," he said sheepishly, "if anyone sees the old man who sells from this pineapple cart, please consider buying from him."

There were smiles from the crowd. Nuwan put back the shelf and pushed the cart away with him, Karadi following. The crowd parted very quickly to let them through, and they made their way to the edge of the jungle where he'd discarded the box and pineapples. The pineapples were all gone but he replaced the box and wheeled the cart to the old man's house. He wasn't sure if the theft had been detected so he put the cart back and left the coin that the monk Mahanama had given him as recompense.

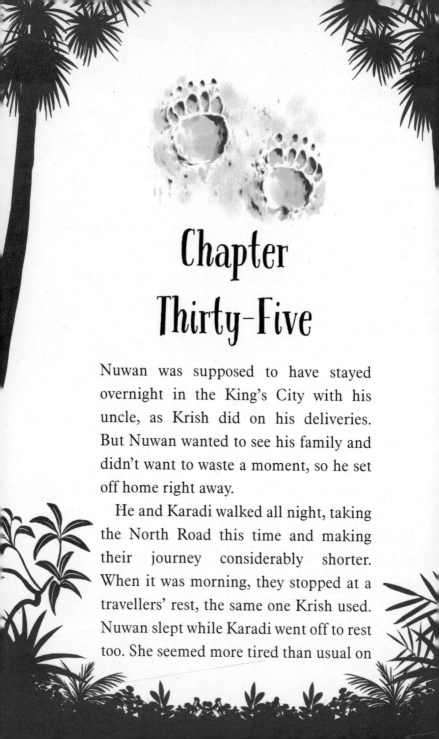

Chapter Thirty-Five

Nuwan was supposed to have stayed overnight in the King's City with his uncle, as Krish did on his deliveries. But Nuwan wanted to see his family and didn't want to waste a moment, so he set off home right away.

He and Karadi walked all night, taking the North Road this time and making their journey considerably shorter. When it was morning, they stopped at a travellers' rest, the same one Krish used. Nuwan slept while Karadi went off to rest too. She seemed more tired than usual on the journey back and her nap times were considerably longer.

When they were close to home, Nuwan left Karadi at her cave. It felt like such a long time ago that he'd taken shelter in the cave and been so terrified of her.

"Goodbye, Karadi," he said. "You're safe now. Thank you for coming with me, and I'll come and visit you soon. If you'd like."

Karadi looked at him solemnly for a while, before turning and squeezing her way into the cave.

Nuwan wasn't sure what their relationship would be like after this. He'd been dreading the goodbye but she'd seemed to take it in her stride. When he left she stayed in her cave and didn't follow him. It was a bittersweet moment. He felt sad, but he knew that she was better off being properly wild and that their friendship couldn't continue as it was.

As he was nearing home his stomach fluttered, full of nerves. He was a real mess, and he was looking forward to seeing his family and having a proper meal and sleeping in his bed. But what if they were furious with him?

When he was within sight of home, he heard his mother scream as she came running out of the house. He was nearly knocked down as she squeezed him tight to her.

"Oh you silly, silly boy!" she said. "What did you do! I'm so glad to see you back safe."

Priya came running out too and wrapped her arms around his legs. And Nuwan's tears flowed faster when his father came down the steps with a yell and hugged him too.

"Come on, come inside," said his father, leading him up to the house. Nuwan wiped his tears and followed him.

Krish came out of the house and stared at Nuwan. He looked gaunt and his eyes were red-rimmed, as if he'd been crying a lot. "Oh, you're OK," he said.

"I am," said Nuwan.

"Good." He gulped. "I need you to be OK, so that I can go back to hating you."

Nuwan laughed, and cried, and Krish did too. Krish disappeared into his room after that. Nuwan knew that was the closest he'd get to a show of affection from his brother for now.

"We were so worried about you," Mother said. "Thank goodness Sani could give us some information about you. We looked on the roads for you but you never came. Every day we prayed for you to get back safely."

Nuwan had the best meal that night. Mother outdid herself in cooking, with all of his favourite foods, and they enjoyed a delicious feast together. And there wasn't a ponyfish soup in sight.

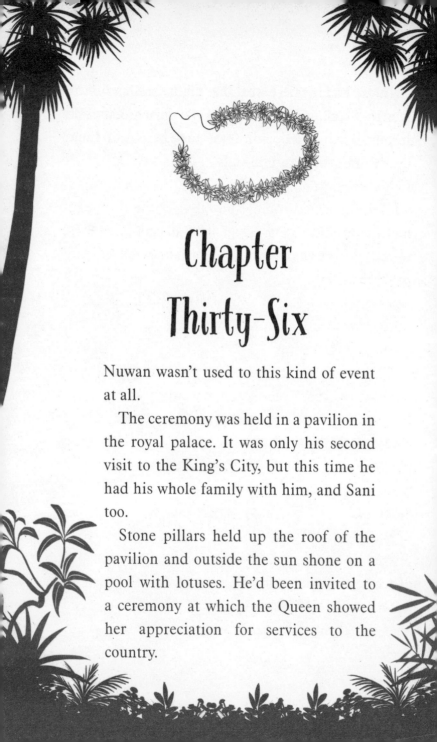

Chapter Thirty-Six

Nuwan wasn't used to this kind of event at all.

The ceremony was held in a pavilion in the royal palace. It was only his second visit to the King's City, but this time he had his whole family with him, and Sani too.

Stone pillars held up the roof of the pavilion and outside the sun shone on a pool with lotuses. He'd been invited to a ceremony at which the Queen showed her appreciation for services to the country.

To his surprise, there were other children there. A trio sitting on the end of the bench had been responsible for hastening the revolution that had overthrown the previous king and installed the Queen in his place. Another three children, one of whom was a foreigner who'd come especially for the ceremony, had found and rescued a historic dagger, and there were two more who'd exposed an island-wide leopard-poaching ring.

Sani and Nuwan felt a bit out of place among such illustrious people, but he wondered if any of the others felt the same.

The ceremony was short but beautiful. When their names were called, each group went up and a short description of what they'd done was read out. The Queen's elephant threw a flower garland on each person, and then the Queen greeted them and handed them a silver plaque that proclaimed them Heroes of Serendib.

And finally it was their turn. Nuwan and Sani walked up and Ananda the elephant draped garlands of fresh flowers round their necks. A soft spray of water fell on Nuwan as the garland dropped and the next thing they knew, they were meeting the Queen herself.

"It's good to see you again, Nuwan," said the Queen. She smiled at them both. "And this must be Sani."

"Yes, Your Majesty."

"I hear you were a big help to Nuwan but you had to stop your journey when you became injured."

Sani blushed. "Unfortunately, yes."

"And you." The Queen turned to Nuwan. "I trust you've accomplished everything you wanted to with your journey?"

"Yes, Your Majesty," he said. And he had. He felt so different from the Nuwan who'd set out so nervously to prove a point to his family.

"Was it hard to say goodbye to Karadi?"

"Not really." He didn't know how to explain it himself. It seemed almost anti-climactic. "I thought she'd find it hard to go back to her old life in the wild. But she did it straightaway."

"Oh, I didn't think she'd find it hard at all," said the Queen. "I imagine she was very eager to get back so that she could have her babies in peace."

"*What?*" said Sani.

"WHAT!" said Nuwan a moment later when he realised what the Queen was saying.

The Queen looked at them amused. "Surely you must have noticed?"

They both shook their heads, at a loss for words.

"Well, good luck to both of you. I hereby declare you Heroes of Serendib." The Queen handed them two shiny plaques that had been passed to her by a very grumpy-looking official. "Thank you, General Siri," she said to him.

Afterwards they all went into the garden for treats.

"This is just wild!" said Sani. "All that time Karadi was with us, and we didn't know she was pregnant."

Nuwan laughed. "I'll never forget her. Ever."

Sani smiled and linked arms with him. "Me neither."

The next morning, on the way home in the cart they'd hired, Nuwan snuggled up next to his mother. She put her arm around him and whispered, "I'm so proud of you, Nuwan. But then I was before all of this, anyway."

Even Krish had come to the ceremony and he'd clapped hard when he thought Nuwan wasn't looking.

Everyone was dozing by the time they drew close to home, but Nuwan couldn't sleep. He was so happy he wanted to savour every minute of this day.

As they were trundling down the road, Nuwan saw a movement in the forest. A familiar black shape was walking across the red soil. Her keen eyes met his and she gave a grunt of recognition as she continued on her way. Nuwan saw two more faces as she disappeared into the trees, the tiny faces of two mini bears who clung to her back.

Nuwan smiled. Karadi and her cubs were safe and busy with their lives.

And so was he and his heart was full.

Acknowledgements

Four books in four years, and what a ride it's been! When I wrote my first book I didn't realise how long I'd spend in this world. It has been a blast!

First of all, thank you to my agent, Joanna Moult, for believing in me and my writing. This is a journey of many highs and lows and I'm so glad to have you as I go through it.

Thank you immensely to Kate Wilson and Kirsty Stansfield for taking on this book and the world of Serendib. This is a place so close to my heart: thank you for helping me bring it to the page. To Maurice Lyon for your thoughtful and patient edits, Nicola Theobald for the cover design, and David Dean for the captivating cover and inside illustrations.

To all at Nosy Crow, especially Rebecca Mason, Sîan Taylor and Hester Seddon. Thank you for being a wonderful team and for all your hard work on my books.

To the US team, including Jonah Heller, Elyse Vincenty, Sara DiSalvo, Darby Guinn and all at Peachtree: thank you for all that you do for my books across the pond.

To my foreign publishers: thank you for the beautiful

books and for taking my words and stories to new audiences. It's truly a privilege to reach readers of other languages across the world.

To all my writing friends near and far, thank you for supporting me and being there in good times and bad: Yasmin Rahman, Hana Tooke, Az Dassu, Rashmi Sirdeshpande, Rachel Huxley, Sophie Kirtley, Hannah Gold, Thushanthi Ponweera and ALL of Swaggers; I'm so lucky to have you.

To all the children I've met at my school visits, both online and in person: you are amazing and I'm sorry I can't use all your names and ideas in my books! One of you guessed the title of this book long before anyone knew it; you know who you are! Shout-out to Year 6 and all of Vita et Pax School in Southgate, Katie Rushton's class and all of Aston Clinton School, and the unforgettable current Year 6 of Driffield Junior School.

To all the supporters of my books I've had the pleasure to know – teachers, librarians, reviewers and booksellers: Chris Soul, Chris Tarrant, Kate Heap, Ashley Booth, Kevin Cobane, Jenny Hawke, Shaahima Fahim, Scott Evans, Bronnie and Bob Mayho, Fern Tolley, Pie Corbett, Tara's Teaching, Emma Perry, Alex Mattimoe, Ayesha Choudhury, Tina Edward Gunawardhana, Mel and Nick, Kirsten Barrett and more; your support has been incredible.

To family and friends across the world in the real Serendib: in the giant footprints of Ananda, the ocean dives of Maalu, the golden gaze of Lokka and the baby bears on Karadi, you are there in spirit in all I've written.

Closer to home, to lovely friends Bushra Sadiq, Saira Shamim and Sharifa Merchant for your encouragement, and to my wonderful daughters Nuha and Sanaa for your loving support.

And finally, as the sun sets on Serendib, thank you to you, dear reader, for everything.

Another great adventure story by
Nizrana Farook, also set on the amazing
island of Serendib!

Read on to find out more!

THE GIRL WHO LOST a LEOPARD

Chapter One

Selvi frowned as the man with the bow and arrow took aim at something in the bushes. She bent low and watched him from her hiding place. What was he hunting?

A whistling thrush called from a tree above him, taking off in a flutter of sleek dark blue. The man twisted in place slightly, as if following a moving target, one eye narrowed in line with the nocked arrow. Next to him, partly obscured by trees, two other figures watched silently.

Far above him in the mountains, Selvi

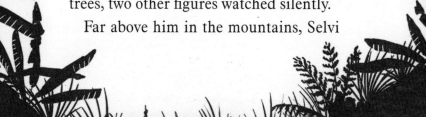

crouched down further. What was going on? She knew the man with the bow by sight, though only vaguely. Jansz was a large man with a big head and chipped teeth, and he and his two companions were known for being troublemakers. If Selvi's mother were here she'd tell her to stay away from them.

From her vantage point, Selvi had an eagle's view of the mountain range. Misty green hills rose around her to varying heights, all covered in a thick wilderness occasionally broken up by exposed rock. Tall eucalyptus trees shot upwards like arrows from the slopes, their balmy fragrance sharpening the breeze. On her right and away to the south lay a vast plain of velvety grassland.

The man exclaimed angrily and lowered his bow. He moved towards the others underneath the tree. Whatever he'd been aiming at, it was gone now.

The men's voices drifted up and it sounded like an animated discussion was going on. Selvi ran light-footedly towards the other side of the mountain, anklets jingling softly. They wouldn't see or hear her here, as long as she didn't make too much noise. She would scale down this side of the mountain and be away from them.

Selvi set off climbing down the bare rock face. She

was adept at this. Even the dangerous climbs that no one else could manage. She was small and light, and that helped as she gripped the rock.

She'd learned to climb by instinct, feeling the sun-hot surface with her feet and arms as she used every hand- or toe-hold to help her down. She knew the type of vines to hold on to, the tufts of bracken that could take her weight best. Her toes curled into foliage and grasped on, as agile as the toque macaques that swung around these parts.

She was partway down the rock face when a movement below caught her eye. She paused and looked down. A clump of yellow daffodil orchids swayed softly among their pointed grassy leaves. Could it be...? Her heart soared. But no, she hadn't seen Lokka in over two weeks. Maybe he'd moved on? It made her sad, but he was a wild animal after all. She shook her head and turned back to the rock face.

But then she caught the soft swish of trees and knew that something was definitely moving below. She held her breath and suddenly caught a glimpse of a sinewy figure with a hint of gold rippling past the foot of a keena tree.

Selvi smiled broadly, her heart singing in her chest. The familiar powerful body, the glossy golden coat with dark rosettes and dabs of softest orange in them. Lokka! She'd missed him so much and was glad to see him sloping around the mountains again.

A whisper floated up in the breeze. Selvi froze as a sudden appalling thought came to her. The men were being very quiet now. *Too* quiet. She scaled back up the rock quickly and crawled to the edge she'd been on before, anklets jingling and elbows scraping the rough ground.

All of a sudden, several things happened at once. An arrow whistled through the air into the bushes. A loud roar from an angry animal echoed up the mountains, followed by a crashing sound coming from the bushes.

Lokka!

Chapter Two

Selvi screamed. They were shooting Lokka! Her dear, strong, magnificent leopard!

The noise echoed over the mountains, reverberating from all sides. The men looked up in alarm.

Selvi fell backwards and scrambled to her feet. One of the men pointed and shouted something indistinguishable. She picked herself up, her heart in her mouth.

The man was now racing up the mountain towards her. Selvi started to

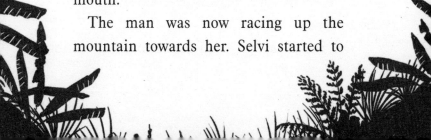

scramble back down the rock face again. What were the men doing?! Everyone knew that hunting leopards had been strictly outlawed by the Queen. The men would be punished severely if they were caught.

Which explained why they were so keen to find her.

Before the men reached the summit, Selvi had made it to the ground, dropping on to a patch of striking purple binara flowers. She thundered down the slopes, anklets jingling as her feet raced through scratchy ferns. But what about Lokka? Could he have been injured? Or worse? She shoved the thought out of her mind. No! He was quick and strong. She'd have to go and find him later and check that he was all right.

But for now she had to save herself.

She stopped momentarily to rip off her anklets. She held the bells tightly in her fingers to muffle the sound as she ran on.

Two men were hurtling down the slope behind her and soon they'd be close enough to see her. Selvi crawled quickly under a low bush. She held her breath as the men stopped nearby, gazing intently over the mountains.

"Where did she go?" said the large man, panting.

The other one peered over the slopes to the valley below. "She couldn't have got very far. We'll find her."

Selvi shrank back as Jansz's massive feet passed close to the bush.

"We'd better!" he snapped, infuriated. "I can't believe we didn't get that stupid leopard again. And I don't want the girl yapping to anyone."

Didn't get the leopard. Selvi exhaled and closed her eyes. Lokka must have escaped. Which was more than she could say for herself…

Jansz hollered to the third man, who was skittering down the slope towards them. "We must find her before she gets home!"

"I can't see her," he replied, holding a hand over his eyes as he scanned the area.

"She'll be hiding close by then," said Jansz. "Spread out around the mountains. We'll get her."

Selvi craned her neck to see one of the men pick up something from the ground.

"Look what I've found!" There was a tinkling as the man threw the small object to Jansz, who caught it in one hand. He held it up – a short chain with a jingling bell at the end.

Selvi shivered and opened her fist. There was only

one anklet clutched in her palm.

"I know who this belongs to," said Jansz. "I'd recognise that annoying sound anywhere. It's Selvi."

Chapter Three

A wave of panic washed over Selvi. They knew her! She'd seen Jansz around the village but didn't think he'd recognise her or know her name. That meant he knew where she lived, or could find out. She stiffened, thinking about Mother alone at home.

"Let's comb the area," said Jansz. "We need to speak to her and make sure she doesn't say anything. If she's difficult we'll just have to talk to the family a little."

Selvi shivered. She knew what that

meant. *Talking* was code for something altogether more threatening. She had to protect her mother from Jansz and his thugs.

The men had split up now, and were moving slowly through the mountains. She didn't want to bump into them. She didn't want to leave them to hurt Lokka either.

Selvi peeked out from the bush again. The men seemed to have moved on a little. She watched as one of them headed away from her down the hill.

Quietly, she crept towards the path leading to her village below. It was a winding mountain track, cool and rain-washed, overhanging with tree ferns and with a sharp drop on one side. It was really hard to see if anyone was coming towards her or approaching from behind. She stumbled and brushed against some overhanging ferns, and a shower of water fell on her.

"Did you hear that?" came Jansz's voice. "That way!"

Selvi changed direction and ran nimbly along a small path that wound steeply upwards. She made it to the top, panting with the effort. To her surprise, there was a house standing in the centre of a neatly swept yard under a large neem tree. Thankfully no one seemed to be home and the front door was closed.

She ran towards the back to find somewhere to hide.

Jansz's voice drifted up from the path below, the trees muffling the sound. "Where did she go now?"

Selvi crept to the back door and pressed herself against it. They wouldn't be able to see her from their position and she couldn't see them either. She prayed they wouldn't notice the little winding track.

"She has to be here! Must be hiding somewhere."

Selvi shivered in her hiding place. The sound of the men's feet swept far and near. A couple of times they came heart-stoppingly close to the bottom of the path, but then they receded again.

Just when she thought they'd moved away and she was readying herself to leave, she heard the sound of light footsteps in the front yard.

Selvi swallowed a scream and flattened herself against the roughness of the back door. The footsteps started to speed up, and suddenly a person rounded the corner of the house and appeared right in front of Selvi.

It was a boy, about her age. He stopped short and let out a yelp of surprise.

"Shh!" whispered Selvi fiercely, recognising him. He was a boy from school, Amir. And, just her luck, one of the mean ones. She guessed that this was his house. "Keep your voice down!"

He stared at her in astonishment. His meanness seemed to have deserted him due to shock. "Why?" he said.

"Just please do," she implored, before he talked too much. The men might be lurking close by. Then more politely, and by way of explanation, she whispered to him, "I don't want people to know I'm here."

"What people? There's no one around," said Amir, although thankfully he'd dropped his voice.

He frowned suddenly and, much to Selvi's horror, said, "Oh wait, who's that?"

Laboured footsteps sounded at the front of the yard, as if someone was trudging up the track.

It was one of the men!

Amir went and stood at the side of the house, watching where the top of the track came up to the front yard. Selvi was immobile with shock.

"Hey, boy," the man said, his voice shaky from the climb. It was Jansz! He was here, just feet away from Selvi. She couldn't see him from where she stood, but she sensed the urgency in his voice. "Have you seen a girl run this way?"

Chapter Four

Amir's eyes swivelled immediately to look at Selvi, cowering in the doorway. Selvi shook her head hard.

Jansz came closer. Selvi could hear him now, breathing heavily, though he was still thankfully hidden by the side of the house.

"Well?" said Jansz to Amir. "It's not a hard question, is it? Have you seen her?"

Amir just stood there, his eyes darting all about the place as if wondering how to answer.

"I have a coin if you've seen anything

useful for me," said Jansz's voice, and he must have shown Amir something that made his face light up.

No! Selvi mouthed. *Please don't.*

Amir dragged his eyes away from Jansz and scratched his head. "Er, no. I haven't seen any girl. But I'll keep an eye out."

Selvi closed her eyes in relief.

"Good," said Jansz. He shuffled off, his footsteps rustling slowly down the track.

Selvi stood motionless for a while until all sounds of him had died away. She felt faint with relief once he was gone. She leaned her head back on the door and looked up, exhaling noisily.

"Thank you," she said to Amir, who was scuffing his toe on the sandy ground.

"What does he want with you?" asked Amir.

Selvi hesitated. She didn't really want to tell him, but she felt she owed him an explanation. "I saw him and his thugs try to kill a leopard."

Amir's eyes goggled. "Out here?"

Selvi nodded. It was acceptable to kill leopards that strayed into villages and posed a threat to humans, but going out to the wilderness to hunt one was a punishable offence.

He looked thoughtful for a moment, then shrugged

and moved to stand in front of her expectantly.

"Is there anything you want?" she said, confused.

He pointed to the door behind her. "Just to get into my house."

"Oh, right." Selvi blushed and moved aside.

Opening the door, Amir gave her a half-smile and went inside. Since it was safe to leave, Selvi went round to the front of the house and made her way back down the tiny mountain track. Trees of twisty branches lined one side, their trunks festooned with waterlogged mosses. The air smelled of clean mountain rain and freshly dug earth. A green lizard, its nose shaped like a leaf, looked up at her from a low branch.

Now to get home and to Mother without being seen by Jansz and his men, who were probably still lurking about somewhere. Selvi was thankful that Amir hadn't told on her. He'd seemed nicer without his friends around, but she still had the uneasy feeling she shouldn't have told him about the men and Lokka the leopard.

Chapter
Five

Selvi ran all the way home. She needed to get there before Jansz did. Her feet flew down the mountainside to the village below. Unlike Amir, who lived in the middle of nowhere, she lived in a hamlet made up of a dozen houses. This was how it was in this remote part of Serendib – a few hamlets scattered throughout the mountains, as well as remote, isolated dwellings tucked away among the peaks.

Selvi took her usual shortcut and squeezed through scraping branches on to the roof of her house, which was on a path lower than the wilderness behind. She dropped down to the ground at the front door and stood up, dusting her hands. She stepped back in fright when she noticed someone was there.

It was her uncle, Kandaraja, and he was staring at her in contempt.

Selvi groaned under her breath. Of all the bad luck! Why did he have to be visiting right now?

Just then, Jansz and one of his men came running round the corner. Uncle looked up at the noise and started when he saw who it was.

Selvi's heart was beating wildly. Uncle was bad enough on his own, always haranguing Mother about her parenting and Selvi's wildness. If the men started hassling Kandaraja about what happened on the mountainside, he'd come down even harder on her and she'd never be allowed out again.

She wanted to speak, but didn't know what to say, how to explain the situation. But for some reason she couldn't understand, Jansz and his goon looked at each other and then took to their heels. They disappeared down the path and round a bend, Jansz thumping heavily at the back.

Uncle turned to face Selvi. "Do you know those men?"

She shook her head silently. She wasn't sure if it was a lie, exactly, but she didn't really know anything about them. Other than the fact that they liked to kill harmless animals.

"Good. Stay away from them. They're good-for-nothings." Uncle Kandaraja smoothed down his immaculate full-white shirt and sarong.

Selvi's mother came to the door. "Brother," she said. "Sorry, were you waiting long? I was washing some clothes at the back and didn't hear you."

Uncle Kandaraja didn't answer but sighed, going past her into the house without invitation and settling himself down on the reed-woven chair.

Selvi followed him, dreading the conversation. Her uncle was her mother's much older brother. He was big on respectability, and what one should and shouldn't do, and keeping up appearances. Uncle was always interfering in their lives, and it annoyed Selvi that her mother always meekly listened and never stood up for herself.

"Get me something to drink, Gayathri," said Uncle. Mother went away at once to make him a hot drink.

Selvi bristled, as she always did when he bossed them about. She made to leave.

"Wait," said Uncle, snapping his fingers. "I haven't

finished with you."

Uncle took his time, waiting for Mother to come back while Selvi stood there twiddling her thumbs and wondering what he had to say this time. She didn't dare leave, not because she was afraid of her uncle but because she didn't want to upset her mother.

Once Mother had handed her brother a cup, she perched nervously on the edge of a chair. Selvi stood there waiting. Uncle sipped slowly. Some small boys went past the open front door, rotating a wheel with a stick on the gravel outside and laughing noisily.

Uncle gestured to Selvi to take his cup once he'd finished. When she'd done so, he looked directly at Mother for the first time. Selvi hesitated on the way to the kitchen when she heard his words. "I was hoping that things would have improved around here. But nothing's changed. The girl still comes and goes whenever she wants."

Selvi's mother flushed. "She just likes being outdoors, Brother. She's a little girl; I think it's good for her to be out playing."

"Playing?" roared Uncle suddenly, making them both jump. "Don't be ridiculous. She's twelve, not five. She should be home attending to her duties with you."

Selvi rolled her eyes inwardly as she put the cup down. No one was sure what these duties were that Uncle kept going on about. She helped her mother with pounding the rice, and sometimes she cooked, or helped with other things around the house. They grew some vegetables too. But she had time to go to school and do other things as well.

Mother nodded. "She does help—"

"Clearly not enough!" Uncle fiddled with the thick gold band on his wrist, which stood out against the dark brown of his skin. Uncle was very rich, from his big shop in town, but his money created a problem for Selvi. He helped Mother financially, and in return he felt he could control everything about their lives.

He looked away suddenly, as if disgusted at the sight of them both, and stood up to go. "I will see you next week then. Although I'm sorry to see you're still not doing an adequate job of bringing the girl up properly."

Any brightness drained out of Mother's face at his parting shot. All his visits were like this. Short and abrupt, they always ended with her mother in tears and full of self-doubt. Uncle went out of the door and they watched him disappear down the path to where his cart would be waiting for him. Soon he'd be rolling off to his big house on a mountain peak.

"Good riddance!" Selvi turned to her mother. "Why do you put up with him?"

"Selvi!" Mother went back into the house wearily. "Don't talk about your uncle that way."

"I know you don't like this either!" Selvi followed her inside. "We don't need him. We get by just fine on the sewing that you do. Stop accepting his money."

Mother pressed a hand to her head. "He won't take no for an answer."

"Of course he won't! He wouldn't get to control our lives then."

"OK, so he is a little strict—"

"Strict!" said Selvi. "This is beyond strict."

"Strict and old-fashioned then," said Mother placatingly. "A bit."

Selvi sighed. "No one thinks like him. Even his own family doesn't agree with him. I don't see why we have to listen."

"He cares about us, Selvi. He's been taking an interest in our lives ever since your father died. He could have left me to struggle alone but, as my older brother, he's thinking of his familial duty and is helping me." She scratched her hands in agitation, as she always did at the end of these visits. "He's probably right. I *am* too soft on you. It would be good for you to go out less and get ready for life."

"You're already preparing me for life! Whatever that is. Stop listening to him." Selvi found the way her mother didn't stand up to Uncle so infuriating!

"Please, Selvi, that's enough. If I'm not doing a good enough job with you I'd rather know. My brother means well." She rubbed her temples and Selvi knew a headache must be coming on. "Go and get some water."

Selvi didn't want to agitate her any more so she went out of the back door to the well, picking up a basin from the kitchen on her way. This was a running argument between her and her mother. Her uncle had too much say in their lives, and it was always to Selvi's detriment. She *knew* Mother wasn't keen on the interference either, but she wanted to keep the peace and wouldn't ever challenge Uncle.

She dropped the bucket in the well and it hit the water with an echoing splash. Selvi pulled on the rope, cranking up the filled bucket via the pulley. She placed the basin on the lip of the well and poured water into it. Picking up the basin, she turned to go.

She started and nearly dropped the basin, sloshing

water down her skirt and feet.

Standing in front of her, in their little backyard, was Jansz.